Boats Against the Current

SCOTT KNIERIM

ISBN: 978-1-962402-54-5

Published by

Fideli Publishing, Inc.
119 W. Morgan St.
Martinsville, IN 46151
www.FideliPublishing.com

Also by Scott Knierim

The Crossing

This book is dedicated to my amazing wife.
Without her, none of my happiness would be possible.

A heartfelt acknowledgement also goes to Dr. David Gugin,
without whom there would be but shadows on the wall.

CHAPTER 1

The sounds of Jimmy Buffett could be heard in the background. Papers were scattered upon the desk that sat in the middle of the office. Spartanly decorated, and compact, it was used by only one person on a day-to-day basis. Correspondence, pens, envelops, and stationary dotted the room. At first glance one could tell this was not like most offices a person would see in a given city or town. However, it was used in much the same way as other offices. One could tell the room had a lack of seriousness about it given the nature of what went on inside its walls. The window that stood on the west side of the room contained a view from the top of a hill overlooking the Mediterranean Sea.

A soft wind blew through the open window, rustling the papers sitting on the desk. A ceiling fan attempted to aid the wind in its conquest of the heat. The walls were dotted with frames holding a collection of artifacts from the life of their owner. It was strange collection ranging from a 125-year-old map of Italy to a frame poster of the Band Pearl Jam. In the corner a signed letter from Sir Edmund Hillary sat in its worn golden frame. The wooden floor gave way a bit with each step. The house itself was quiet old but was holding up well. An old rug had been laid in the middle of the room to soften his step. William thought it could be Persian or found in a back room. Either beginning was a possibility.

William sat at the desk humming to the sound of "Tin Cup Challis" coming from a computer on the table. The sun shined through the window, so he did not have to turn on a single light in order to work. This is how he liked to work. It was simple. No need for a lamp because the sun would do that work. No need for air conditioning because the wind would take care of that too. There was a phone, but it did not do much. There was truly little need for anyone to contact this office. In truth, not many people really knew this was an office at all. Not to fault them. It was located in the front room of a house outside of a small town on the Italian coast. Not bad work if you can get it. He had but one client, and that client was not home very much. William was tanned from head to toe which was unusual for him. Living on the coast of Italy had been good to his complexion. A touch of blond was now blending into his brown hair from many days out on the water. William had settled into his new life quite nicely.

The house was owned by Marcus Fairfield, of the Chicago Fairfields. The history of this particular clan would be enough to fill pages of the Chicago business world. Chicago is where Marcus grew up, and his family was still there. A long line of Fairfields had been in the upper crust of Chicago since the fire destroyed the city. Just the name sounded as if the house would be occupied by a smoking-jacket wearing, wine sipping aristocrat. Although many of his family members were that type of person, the namesake occupant of the house was far from that. Marcus Fairfield had wanted something different than the rest of the Fairfield he called family. His house reflected that fact. It was a simple house that fit in with its simple surroundings. Yet the simplicity hid the fact that Marcus was a man of means. The house sat on the top of a hill overlooking the Mediterranean Sea. It was a story and a half, with yellow paint fading on the outside. The location itself was not one for the faint of heart, or the light of wallet. It had a small drive that connected it to the dirt road about two miles outside of town. There was a path that took tourists from one town to the next almost touching the side yard. Now and then one could here languages from around the world being spoken just yards from the window. However, this was a simple house owned by not so simple of a man.

The inside of the house was nice, but not over the top. With a large inheritance to draw from, Marcus could have put anything he wanted in his home. However, it was not much different than each and every house that dotted the hillside overlooking the water. There had been a few additions since its purchase. The veranda, with its spectacular view, was expected to hold more people. Also, the kitchen, which tends to be small in this area, was enlarged to fit dinner parties. There were three bedrooms, each of which was occupied. One was for Marcus, one for William, and the other for whomever seemed to be passing through at the time. Most of the time there seemed to be someone passing by. Whether it was from the town just down the path, or some old friend from another country.

Since his work was not demanding, William was able to take time in order to just unwind throughout the day. William knew he was kind of living off the money of another. So when he could he tried to make himself useful. William and Marcus had known each other for years. However, he had come to work for Marcus in a very strange way. He had known Marcus from college at the University of Evansville back in the United States. They had ended up pledging the same Fraternity. At Sigma Alpha Epsilon they slowly became friends.

William was quiet, and liked to observe from a distance, and Marcus was the life of the party. His family was wealthy, and well connected, but you would never have guessed it if you talked to him. Marcus had the rare quality of being rich, but approachable. He did not look down on anyone and did not judge people based on money or status. People were drawn to him. He was a natural leader, and throughout his three years in college he was in numerous leadership positions. He was a member of the University's Leadership Academy, student counsel, as well as the executive counsel of the Fraternity.

Then he caught the ailment that affects many with youth and money. He left college to take a look at the world. William stayed to finish his school. Marcus would check back with his friends from faraway places. Given the money was never an issue, there were trips to all corners of the globe.

While William was studying for his Bio-Ethics Final, he would get word that Marcus had done some fishing off of Zanzibar. The mail would come with a post card of wild beaches with a postage stamp of some far-off country.

As time went by, William was applying to Law School and Marcus would be viewing art in Amsterdam. Marcus would travel around the world but would never come back to the United States. William would try and stay in contact with him, but it got more difficult as time went by. Marcus would travel further away, and the letters, e-mails, and contacts got less and less.

The last letter he got said that Marcus was in Italy, and that he was going to stay put for a while. He stated that he had some work to do and was happy to settle down. William was pushing his way through his second year of Law School and trying to figure out how to file a Civil Complaint. There was not much time to reconnect with an old friend. However, for some reason

William had saved that letter with the address of Marcus's place. Maybe there was something deep down inside the told William he may need it someday.

More time went by with nothing from either side of the ocean. William went about his education in the manner he was always expected to do. After three years of hard work William was about to finish school. William liked the law. The legal instinct had always been with William. He knew from an early age, much earlier than those around him, that his talents lay with the law. He had a logical way of thinking that made the legal profession an easy choice. However, once in law school things began to slowly change. Once mixed with others who were going to pursue the law, the law itself seemed less of a worthy goal. The nuts and bolts of practicing law were much different that the thought of one day standing in a courtroom being Atticus Finch. It was not a hard decision the day William decided to walk away.

From time-to-time William would sit in his makeshift office and wonder how he ended up in such a fortunate situation. Always and outdoors person, William would wake up not with a cup of coffee, but with a short jog outside. There were no deadlines, nor were there any rules about when he needed to be at work. Therefore, he was free to just get up with the sun and work the way he wanted. Breaks would mean hiking the path that ran to the next town or walking down the dusty drive to the only road. Either way it gave him time to think and prepare for the day. It was a far cry from the rest of his classmates in law school who would probably start the day with a frantic dash for work, all the while worrying about the next motion deadline, or court case they would have to take on. William saw that life coming and was scared to death. Sitting in class preparing to take the bar exam back in Indiana, all he could think about was a way to get out. The test day crept closer and closer with William spending more time riding his bike as far as it could take him rather than try and memorize another set of rules regarding Administrative Law.

The Indiana Bar Exam was actually two full days of test taking. The first day were endless hours of multiple-choice questions tackling all aspects of the law? Once you ran that gauntlet, then you were in store for another day of essays. William finished the first day of testing and ran as fast as he could out the doors. He wondered around downtown Indianapolis for hours after the test. He sat on the steps of the soldier's and sailor's monument on the circle and watched the movement of the people. All of them seemed to be in a hurry. Sitting on the steps in the middle of the city, William wanted to run. He wanted to go anywhere. He wanted to be anyplace but where he was. He walked back to his hotel thinking about places he could go. Thoughts of running off to Paris, or Central America ran though his head. When he got back to his hotel, only blocks away from his testing the next day, William started to rethink. He stood in the elevator waiting for his floor thinking that this may be what everyone goes through in his situation. He just needed some rest, maybe a drink, and to just get through the next day.

He did manage to get through the next day. William was one of the first to finish the test and bolt out the door. He drove to his family home only a few miles away. It was there that he realized he needed to get away. It was an exhilarating feeling. As though a weigh was being lifted from his shoulders. He had spent his whole life marching towards this point, and now once he had reached his destination, he could only feel emptiness. So with the benefit of youth, he told his family that he was going away for a while. Saying that he needed a break from the pressures of getting through the bar exam, he took some money that he had saved up in the bank and bought a ticket to Italy. It was the only place that he knew someone and could get away from the life he was about to lead.

All of that was behind him now. He had stored that memory far back in his mind. Sitting in the office of his old friend's house William usually did not spend much time thinking about how he got there. He was happy that he was there, and that was all he needed. After he had been gone for a while, he had let his family know where he was, and that he might not be home for a while. Other than that it did not take him long to settle down into his newfound life. Surprisingly, not long after his arrival he had met a girl, and they fast became something of a couple. Maria was a local girl with beautiful brown hair, and brown eyes. They started slow, but recently have started to spend more and more time together. She was a local officer in the town, and someone that Marcus had known for a while. If the incredible scenery were not enough to keep him here, a girl like Maria surely could.

After some time the town became home. It had been there since Roman times and was awash in history. The families in the surrounding hills had been there for centuries. There were grapes growing of the slopes of the hills surrounding the town. Train tracks ran outside of the town next to a small road. Most people got to the town by train. There was a path that ran along the sea cliffs that connected several towns along the coast. Marcus' house was near one of those paths. William got to know the locals and learned enough Italian to get by. He never missed life in the States. The movement was too fast, and there was not as much depth as he found here. Not that he had found paradise. Every now and then he would run into what Marcus would call "issues". After a bit of adventure, things would turn back to normal. It was this normal life that William wanted to continue as long as he could. He was young and did not have anything particular to attend to. So he had the luxury to sit about in a seaside village and attend to the workings of his friends' "issues".

One of the main jobs William had was to go through Marcus' mail every day. Surprisingly, for a man who lived out in the middle of nowhere and did not seem to want to be around much of anyone, he received a good amount of mail. Not only that, but the mail would come in from all around the world. At first William thought that it was crazy to deal with paper mail. With e-mail at the click of a button, it was like dealing with communication in 1975. However, Marcus insisted. He did not like computers and told William if someone wanted to get a hold of him, they would have to do it the hard way. Since he was the boss William opened the mail. A good amount of it had to do with investments and dealing with financial issues. Marcus did not seem to have much interest in what was going on with his money, as long as it was there when he needed it.

William set about making sure everything was in order to keep that money being there. Marcus wanted everything to be done quickly and did not have the patience for looking after money. William's legal background helped put the brakes on Marcus' money issues. Outside of that there was a good amount of correspondence regarding some of the projects that Marcus would support around the world. He had always been kind of a crusader for the unfortunate. William always suspected it stemmed from the fact that Marcus had grown up with money and felt a bit guilty about it. Marcus had spent time traveling around the world, and he did not do it in high style. He would go about walking down dirt roads to villages in Costa Rica, and Panama. He would fly into India, and just set off to some far-off place with no real reason. With that experience, and a good amount of money, it was not unusual for someone like him to be involved such things.

Money would go out everywhere, and to a number of people. When he was able William would try and sit down with Marcus to figure out why money was going where. Marcus was not one to give many specifics.

"I just need to know the basics on why we are wiring $20,000 to South Africa?" William would ask trying to get information out of his friend.

"I have a friend in need of some money down there," would be Marcus' reply. "I think he can do some good with it,"

That would be the back and forth between the two of them each time William would ask. He would tell Marcus that he was only trying to look after his money and do his job. Marcus knew that, and never got mad at William asking where the money was going. However, he still did not let William in on it. It was just as well William thought. It was his money, and William's only job was to look after what Marcus wanted to do.

William had been noticing that there was a lot of money going to Central America. There would be letters from individuals in Nicaragua, or Costa Rica. Some of them would be in English so William could take care of them, but the rest would be in Spanish. William did not know Spanish, and neither did Marcus. Therefore, William would have to find someone who spoke Spanish to translate the letters in order to tell Marcus what they were. Once that was done, he would take the letter to him, and ask what he wanted done. Marcus would study them for a bit, and without explanation tell William to do one thing or another.

"Take $5,000 and wire it to Mr. Janka in Rivas," Marcus would tell him without looking up from the letter. "Make sure it can get there in the next 24 hours."

"Is it important?" William asked.

"Important enough to need it in the next 24 hours," Marcus would reply without another word.

William did not think that Marcus was involved in anything wrong, so he never pushed. Marcus was a close friend, but there were certain places William was not willing to go. So William would do as he was told. Nothing seemed to be too much out of the ordinary. Yes, there was money going around the globe for one thing or another, but Marcus was a wealthy man. It was just something that wealthy men did.

So day after day, and week after week, William would go about his part time job of keeping track of Marcus. After a few hours of work he would be done from the day, and head outside to the Italian coastline. He did not have much but spending days at the water's edge made up for most of it. The weather was good most of the year, and William did not have to bother with big changes in the seasons like back in Indiana. The winters were mild, with one needing a light jacket, or sweater, to go outdoors. The spring came quickly, and the summers were long and warm. It was a pleasant place to live.

Maybe that life would not last forever, but William was content with not rocking the boat. Soon after the sun started to set the citizens of Sevena would come out and start to socialize. The bars and restaurants opened up, and people gathered in the streets for the evening. Many nights William would meet up with Maria and head to the Blue Marlin for a few drinks. Marcus would come down from the house every now and then. However, he was not an every night guest in town.

William loved the town life. One could grab a bite of fruit, and some fresh bread, off a cart in the morning, and sit by the small harbor watching the fishermen tend to their nets. It was a scene out of a storybook, and William was allowed to live it. His Italian was still a bit rusty, so William was not able to sit around and talk with many of the locals. A good number of them spoke English, but many of those chose not to. William could respect that and vowed to spend more time learning Italian. Maria told him time, and time again, that she would teach him. William did not like the thought of spending more time sitting around learning. He had done that for years. He promised her that soon he would get serious and learn. For now, he would just have to get by and the bits and pieces he had picked up. Life was good, but William knew that things do not always last forever.

CHAPTER 2

The sun had been up for a few hours, but William was still away from his desk. One of the best parts of being an assistant to a friend were the office hours. In reality there were no office hours. He had decided to go to the water before looking over his day's work. The Mediterranean was refreshing. The salt content was so high that it was not too terribly difficult to lay and float. Rarely was there even a person in sight once William reached the water. That was one of the best parts. Having time to himself each day was something William cherished. Laying in the water he would let his thoughts linger. The sun was just starting to make its way across the sky. William could see boats miles out on the water slowly making their way across the sea. He was content to let it all pass and stay in place as long as he could.

Once the sun started to warm, William knew that it was time to head back up to the house. Thinking that there was nothing particularly important to do in the day, William took his time to get back to the house. William floated in the water looking out at the water one last time before moving. He tried not to think that his life was like a vacation every day.

William gathered his clothes and toweled off. The path leading up to the house was itself a stair step workout. Walking into the house William tossed his towel on the chair and made his way into the office. The mail from the previous day had been sitting on his desk. There seemed to be the same amount of the letters as any other day. There were a couple of e-mails waiting for his response, but nothing that would tax his energy too much. William left the office and went to change. Once in his room he put on a pair of linen pants and a t-shirt. There was a strict no need for shoes policy set up in the house. Given that he was the only employee, it was not hard to enforce.

After returning to the office and sitting down in his chair, William looked over the letters in front of him. One particular caught his attention. It was a battered small envelope with a stamp that included a toucan, and a palm tree. It had been sent from Costa Rica about 10 days before. It was not unusual for Marcus to get a letter from Costa Rica, or from any far-flung place for that matter. However, the writing on the front look rushed, and unlike the formal letters requesting funding William had seen before.

Marcus was gone for the day, out for a trip up the coast. He never knows when, and where Marcus would appear. If there was anything important William would have to take care of it. William ripped open the letter, and sat back in this chair to read:

> *I hope this letter finds you soon. There is trouble. I do not know how badly, but I am in it knee deep. I will be on the island Paraiso Perdido. I need you here fast. Things going downhill quickly. Find the Leopard.*
>
> *Chris*

William had seen a lot of letters, but this one he could not quite get. He read it over a few times and thought about what to do. There were a lot of crazies out there that would love to have a rich guy bail them out. He had not heard anything about the Leopard before, but people called themselves a lot of different things. William wonder who the hell Chris was. Marcus would leave him out of the loop on many things until the last minute. There had already been a surprise trip to Africa the William would have liked to forget. The phrase that struck him as odd was 'need you here fast'. Marcus was known to help many people in need. However, that did not mean that he just dropped everything.

Walking into the kitchen to get something to drink, William put the letter on the table. He could call Marcus and tell him but did not want to bother him with something stupid. Besides, most of the time Marcus would not answer the phone while away. Taking care of this type of things without asking the boss was the reason he was here. He wandered back into his office and looked at the other letters. They were the usual collection of requests for money, or personal correspondence that Marcus let him take care of. William was a little embarrassed to be responding to Marcus's personal mail as though he was Marcus, but it just came with the territory. No one really knew Marcus' handwriting. William would write out the response's longhand. Marcus had given him a lot of latitude regarding how he could respond.

"Don't make me sound like an idiot," aas really the only thing Marcus told him.

Therefore, the responses gave William a dose of creative writing time. Polite refusals for some, and quick affirmations for others. All in a day's work. However, he could not get the letter from Chris out of his mind. William walked back into the kitchen and picked up the letter. He had Marcus' little-known cell phone number that may or may not work, depending on where he was. He looked at the phone trying to figure out if this was the time to call. He decided it was not.

William did not like finding himself in the trials and tribulations of Marcus' life. He knew enough of the things Marcus was up to, and William sometimes kept his distance. Looking out toward the water William tucked the letter into his pocket and decided to give it some time. The letter sounded urgent, but he never knew what to believe. He returned to his desk to look over the other packages, and letters, Marcus had received for the day. However, the letter in his pocket kept popping up in his mind. Not long after he sat down, William's curiosity got the best of him. He grabbed his iPad and started to look up The Leopard. He got nothing.

"I don't know what I was supposed to find," he said out loud to no one.

After switching the iPad off William sat in the empty house wondering about his next move. It was his job to keep track of these things and notify Marcus if anything came up. The letter seemed as though something had come up. William tried to think back to other conversations he had with Marcus, or other letters he had seen, but could not think of a Chris in Costa Rica. William knew that not all of Marcus' mail came through him. He also had a suspicion that Marcus would use e-mail, or take calls, that he did not know about. All of it was wrapped up in the same package.

William did not like that the day had gotten off to a bad start. So William did want any good ex-pat in Europe would do. He got up and headed down to the local watering holed to clear his head. Maybe down at the Blue Marlin he would find some answers. At least he knew he would find a couple of beers. It was almost lunch time, early enough for a pre-lunch beer.

William made his way down the path that lead to town. He liked the idea of a walkable life. Even though the walk might take fifteen or twenty minutes he did not mind. The weather was usually nice, and the view could not be better. The path made its way meandering toward the little town. On one side William could look out over the water and see fishing boats coming in from their morning work. On the other side were rolling hills off as far as the eye could see.

Town was its usual sleepy self when William came walking down the main, and only, road. The fruit stands that dotted the way were closing up after serving their morning purpose. Shops were open but were hardly straining at the workload. William passed by a Gelato store and made his way past the drug store to where the Blue Marlin stood. He walked under the sign with a fish that gave the place its name and sat down at the bar. There was only one other person in the place, and things did not seem as though they were going to get much busier. He ordered a Moretti and took a drink. His mind wandered back to the letter that he saw that morning. He had put it in his pocket while he thought about what to do. However, now the letter was burning a hole in his pocket. He had not seen a letter that spelled out trouble like that one did. The light from the front window shone down on the bar as he thought about what to do with the letter. He pulled it out of his pocket to read it again. If it was a cry for help, he knew that something needed to be done. He could not shake the contents of the letter, and the tow questions that stumped him. Who was Chris, and who was The Leopard?

CHAPTER 3

Indeed, things had gone downhill quickly. The cell that Chris now called home was a seven foot by eight-foot concrete block with a small window looking out toward the side of another building. Officially, he was being housed at the Government's Investigational Headquarters in Palla, the small capital of the island of Paraiso Perdido. Since he was a citizen of the United States there was a bit of confusion as to where to place him during his investigation period. Frankly, the place did not hold too many foreign nationals. Usually, if someone from a different country got picked up by the police it was because of a few too many Margaritas. They would sober up, pay a fine, and be on their way. This time was different. Orders came from the top that this American was to be held at Headquarters and kept there until further notice. Only one man could give an order like that, and if that man made the order everyone knew that it should be obeyed.

The Col. did not like anything that could bring unwanted attention to administration of the island. The local population was under control, and most of the tourists from Europe were surprisingly complacent to lay under umbrellas drinking cheap alcohol. It was the Americans he always worried about. Americans had a propensity to draw attention to themselves, or whatever it was they were doing. Some people liked them because they spent a lot of money. Some people hated them because they asked a lot in return. Of course, there were times when they got into trouble. They would then call on every government agent, United States or local, to help them with their plight. There had been countless numbers of college students brought in on minor drug violations that seemed to be handled directly by the US State Department. However, the Col thought he had something different this time. The man sitting in the jail cell was not some college co-ed, or rich kid, that would call daddy to get him out of her unfortunate situation. There was risk to holding onto this one, but the Colonel did not know of any other way to handle it. The risk was worth it this time.

Even though Chris could not see it. The sun shone down on the main square of Palla, and its palace of government, that morning. As the seat of the island government, the palace of government was home of the Governor of Paraiso Perdido. It was a bit ironic that the man in charge of the government of the island was addressed as The Col. Many noting how difficult it must have been for him to attain such a rank in a nation that had not had a standing army since the late 1940s. For the few Americans on the island a comparison to Col. Sanders of Kentucky Fried Chicken came naturally. However, that is where the similarities ended. The Col. was dead set on making the island his own fiefdom. He had put in place many of the apparatus of a dictatorship. There was a section of secret police headed by a trusted friend who reported directly to him. Once the police were under his control, the natural next move was an expansion of the island prison to accommodate the new prisoners who had violated the brand-new laws against denouncing the government. Those new laws were written by the Colonel and were sold as a protection of the people. The island Counsel were given bribes and promises of more to come. In the end the laws were enacted, and the Colonel was in control.

As the Colonel looked down upon the streets of the city in the early morning few people were milling about. He had been up most of the night worrying about overtures being made by the Central Government back on the mainland. For the past few years, the Government had left him alone. Early on he had been democratically elected by the people of the island. Back on land the Central Government gladly handed off the administration of a notoriously difficult island. Their hands-off approach led the Colonel to consolidate his power and bend the local government to his liking. However, it was never easy to control everything. He was on a slippery slope trying to hold his ground. However, assistance came from an unexpected place to distract the Central Government from his problem little island.

The economic downturn had been tough for the country. The Government of most countries were just trying to keep their heads above water. A few unhappy islanders were nothing compared to the problems of running a country. The island fared no better. Tourism and shipping were the main source of income for the islanders. When the tourists stopped coming, and the ships got fewer and fewer, the people started to get restless. The Colonel was keen to sense the change in attitude and used it for his advantage. He blamed the people's problems on the Central Government, too many restrictions on local rule. He blamed it on the foreign interest, which there were relatively few, who were exploiting the island. The people loved it. Since it was not their fault, they had no problem with the Colonel taking a few of their liberties, in exchange for the promise of better times. It had been three years now, and the liberties were fewer, and the problems much the same.

As his grip on power tightened a small, but vocal minority appeared. The Colonel set his sights on them immediately. They had the audacity to speak out against him. This the Colonel would not tolerate. Any whiff of trouble from the Central Government, could send his whole scheme crashing down. Therefore, he acted like most dictators who came before him. He jailed those who spoke out. Once the voices were quieted, there would be less likelihood of someone from the mainland poking around his island. Each week more and more people would be taken in for questioning. These individuals would be spending anywhere from hours to months in the "processing unit." Their families and friend told little about their fate. From the beginning he targeted the poor. There were few people on the island that had wealth. Those who did found it easy to deal with the Colonel, and he made sure that they were placated. It was the poor who would have to be looked after. They would not have the resources to fight and would not be noticed by many on the mainland. If he could show these people, he was not a person to be challenged, then the rest would fall in line.

Standing on the balcony overlooking the square the Colonel could just make out the building down the street that was his Central Processing Center. As it stood there were dozens of men sitting in cells on his order. As the numbers grew, so did his exposure to problems. Throughout the night he had sat with a small circle of advisors to figure out how to stem the tide of opposition. More and more voices were calling out, and it was getting tougher to keep them all quiet. Sooner or later he would run out of space in his jail. Worse, if the mainland got involved his whole system would come crashing down around him, and it could be his butt sitting in a cell. The Colonel was determined to do whatever it took to keep that from happening.

Behind the Colonel the doors to his main office were opened to let in the morning air. One of the few men that stuck around after the nightlong meeting was a close friend. His name was Pinocce Gravis, and he was the Colonel's right-hand man. Also, he was the only man the Colonel really trusted. Strutting out to the balcony Pinocce wiped the sweat off his already heated brow. He had grown up on the island like most of its inhabitants, poor. When the Colonel came to power, he saw his opportunity to take it. Early on he saw what the Colonel was going to do to his home. He made his deal with the devil and joined the party.

"I like the quiet of the morning," the Colonel stated as he scanned the square down below. "This is the only time of peace that I have in a day." The Colonel gave a distant stare out above the buildings. The sun had begun to rise, and the light had started to break up the shadows down below.

"The disturbance will not just go away," Pinocce stated. "We can only keep these people quiet for so long."

"We just need more time."

"That is something that we may not have." Both men stood in silence for a minute. Neither had the answers they were looking for. A long night without sleep had made them slow and tired.

"There is much to do Colonel," Pinocce told him as he began to leave. "Go and get some sleep, and I will report back to you in a couple of days." With this, Pinocce took his leave. His statement did not seem to make the Colonel feel any better.

After a few minutes, the Colonel returned to his office and poured a tall glass of Gin from the Tumbler on his desk. It was incredibly early in the morning for such a large drink, but since he had not slept the night before he considered it just another in a long line of drinks that had not stopped. He sat down in his high-backed chair and took a long sip of the Gin. The burning of his throat gave him the instant jolt he needed to keep going. He turned his chair around so he could look out the window across the way to the Holding Center. He knew that he had made a decision that could jeopardize his power and his freedom. It had been an impulsive move that he had regretted almost right after he gave the order. However, the deed was done, and there was no going back. He knew that there were people waiting on this next move. Time would not stop, and people cannot be held in jail forever. He sat in his office alone and pondered his next step.

Inside the cell Chris sat and thought about how he had ended up in such a unique situation. He had never been in a jail before. He felt the sensation that all inmates feel when in jail. Time slows down. Everything that a person fills his day within order for time to move has been taken away. Sitting there in his cell all he really had right now was time. He had not been let out of his cell for three days.

Twice daily a guard came around and gave him his meals. The food was not as bad as he thought it would be, but it was not great either. He had not seen many other inmates during his stay. It seemed as though the guards were trying to keep everyone away from each other. He had seen two men in passing when they were taking him to his cell. They did not look like hardened criminals.

In fact, when Chris saw them, he was a bit surprised. They looked like a couple of teachers at a local high school. It was hard to sleep on the ground with only a small blanket, and no pillow. Sleep and thought were the only two things he was allowed to have in his cell. The slowness of the time allowed him to sit and think about the months leading up to his arrest. He was not the type of person to end up on the floor of a jail cell. However, even as he sat alone in his cell, he was not too surprised that he had ended up there. There are always consequences to action. He made the choice to act, and now he was suffering the consequences. He laid down on the cool floor and looked up at the ceiling. It was cracked and broken, like most of the rest of the building. For a moment he wondered if the whole thing could come crashing down. He had no control over what would happen next, so he tried to lose himself in thoughts of the past. He knew that would be easier than trying to worry about the future.

Chris closed his eyes and thought back to where this all might have started. He thought back to how he got to Costa Rica in the first place. The memory took him back to a School in the middle of America.

CHAPTER 4

The University of Kansas had one of the best Spanish history programs in the country. The sprawling campus in Lawrence was home to thousands of students making headway on their respective careers. Chris came there with the same intentions. He had been interested in Spanish history since his undergraduate days at the University of Evansville. There he had majored in History and Education with the hopes of someday becoming a teacher. After a few years in the classroom he wanted more. He spent a year in Spain learning the intricacies of the language and culture, and then settled down in the heartland to learn more about a culture thousands of miles away.

The interest in Spain and its history never left him, but as he went through his education the pull of the Spanish speaking cultures interested him. Mexico and Latin America was a lot closer, and cheaper, than Europe. He took advantage of the University sponsored trips to Central and South America. He traveled through Bolivia and made a few trips to Honduras. However, his real love was for Costa Rica. It was not easy to get a trip to Costa Rica given that it is one of the most beautiful places on the planet. Only a few graduate students each year got to go. During his third year he managed to tag along on a research vacation with one of his professors. He got to travel around the country in a van visiting with Ticos from all walks of life. He loved the beauty and simplicity of life in Costa Rica. The people were warm and friendly, and the country was amazing to look at.

After that Chris was hooked. He was able to scrap together a few bucks, and head down to the West Coast of Costa Rica a few times before graduation. Each time he spent a bit more time and got a bit closer to the people of the country. The country was easy to love. Leaving the cold wind-swept plains for a lush tropical garden was enough for anyone. The transition was made easier by the fact that Chris spoke fluent Spanish and was at ease with the culture of a Central American country.

Chris fell in love with the diversity of the country. One could explore volcanos among the peak of the central peaks. Only a couple hours later one could be sitting on the beach looking out over the Pacific. Chris decided to make as many trips as his meager stipend would let him.

On his last trip as a student he went to the island Parido Praso and made a few friends. The island had a much different attitude than the mainland. Where in the mainland the people were easy going and outspoken, there seemed to be wariness about the people who live on the island. As if they were being watched everywhere they went.

Chris spent a few weeks talking to people about living on the island and quickly found out that this was not some laid back island. Being naturally inquisitive, Chris wanted to know more. He decided to stay on the island for a bit longer. Chris was taken in by a small group of people who seemed to be trying to do something about trouble. He started to understand what was going on.

The government had clamped down on anyone who would questions its goings on. People were being taken to jail, with no word on why, or when they would be returned. There was a large number of police being deployed in the streets even though there was no real trouble to deal with. Newspapers were being shut down or gagged. All of it was in the name of security. The people were scared, and many did not want to risk being caught up in it by speaking out. Chris spent an extra three weeks on the island. He told the powers that be back in Kansas that he was finishing up some research and begged for more time. He was told he needed to get back.

Chris hated to leave just as he was getting involved, but he told his new friend that he would be back. He was not easy, but after seeing all of this Chris had to leave and return to the United States. With his studies almost completed he knew what he wanted to do. He had never been one for adventure, but he figured it was now or never. So soon after graduating with a PH d in History he was back on the island and ready to do something. He just did not know what it is he was supposed to do.

Soon enough he was running around with people who wanted to push back. He spent days in the backrooms of store which doubled as the print shop for a newsletter bashing the government. It was a small operation, but one that was gain readership. Many were too afraid to speak out in public because of the increased security. They had been on the island their whole lives. Chris discovered how things were not always this bad. Everyone kept saying how things changed once the Governor came to power. What they needed was someone to see what they local government was doing. It would be dangerous work for any of the locals. However, Chris thought since he was an American that he would somehow be spared any trouble. Chris volunteered to be a pair of eyes and ears for the group. It would be easy for him to hang around looking like just another American looking for paradise. That was enough for a while, but even Chris got tired of being quiet. He started to attend government meetings and report back to the opposition. To make matters worse he spoke out at some of the meetings. Given that he was fluent in Spanish many people did not know what to make of him. Here was an American in their midst complaining about treatment of people he hardly knew. Little did he know the people in charge were making sure they knew of him? He was being followed, and most of his activity was watched. He knew that the local government had taken an interest in him. However, he still thought that he would be treated lightly given that he was an American. After a few days of the uncomfortable feeling that he was not alone he decided to create an insurance policy. He knew the road he was heading down could end up badly. So, he wrote a short letter to an old friend. At least someone on the outside would know where he was if something bad did happen.

Maybe it was the naiveté of an American in a foreign land, or maybe he had just pushed his luck, but it was not long before Chris ended up in the crosshairs. One day he had decided to attend a local meeting concerning the government's plan to knock down a building and build a new one.

It was an obvious bribe job, in that the owner had given money to the Col. In return for the permission to kick all of his low paying tenants out. He was in line to make a bundle on the new development. However, the people involved wanted to fight back.

Chris attended the meeting which had become heated. Person after person complained about the shoddy nature of how the process had been handled, and the hardship it was on the people who lived there. If it would have been left at that nothing would have happened. That was not enough for Chris. His blood was up, and he wanted to speak out. He strode up to the front and addressed the crown in a way that the government was not ready for. At first the people looked on with a bit of confusion in regard to this American that was speaking for them against their own government. However, soon he was making sense to them, and they started to cheer. Unfortunately, they cheered a little too much, and a little too loud. As an excuse to stop the meeting and disperse the crowd, the police came in to "restore order", and placed Chris under arrest for in sighting a riot. Not that anyone had been rioting or would have gotten even close given the three to one ratio of police to citizen. However, given the natural lack of imagination of governments and police everywhere, they went back to the tired old cliché of in-sighting a riot. He was hauled down to the Detention Center. There was no hearing, no judge, just sitting in a cell and waiting.

The first night in his cell Chris sat thinking about whether help was on the way. He knew that the local people he had met could do little. It would be too much of a risk for them to stick their neck out for him. He should have known from the beginning that something like this could happen. He had told his family where he was going, but nothing about what he would be doing once he got there. Chris was not overly excited about explaining why he ended up in a jail in Costa Rica.

There was a small hope that the U.S. Government would step in, but Chris did not know how much that could help. He ran his hands through his hair thinking about the various ways things could turn out. There were moments of terror when he thought about how bad things could be in a Central American jail. However, he knew that in order to get through this ordeal he would have to get control over himself and keep calm. He now wished that he would have put more information into the letter he sent out. He did not know if the letter would even make it out of the country, let alone all the way across the world. Sitting on the floor of his cell he looked at the ceiling and wondered if Marcus could even help. He hoped that the letter would find him, and that he would be able to find the person that Chris knew could help in this type of situation. All he had to do was find the Leopard.

CHAPTER 5

Trying to find Marcus in the middle of the day was an impossible task most of the time. While best friends, with an employee-boss element mixed in, it was still difficult to nail Marcus down. He would go off to who knows where at any moment. It was William's job to keep everything running while he was gone. Then he would just pop in, and act like he had never left. Marcus hated e-mail and cell phones. He would rather just live as if the world were in the 1980's. However, there were still ways to get a hold of him. People knew people that knew how to get to him. William just put the word out there and waited. Since reading the letter William sent word that he needed to talk to Marcus now. All he could do now was wait.

Waiting for William was not bad. After his relatively easy workday, he would meet up with his girlfriend Maria. They would get a bite to eat at one of the many small out of way places that dotted Sevena. There was skinny dipping in the water, or just hanging around the house together. William could not get enough of his brown hair, and brown eye beautiful girl. She was a police officer for the local government. Therefore, not only could she keep him out of trouble, but know most of the business going on in their small town. Their relationship had been easy from the start. She was a person that William could get close to. However, there had always been the question of where the relationship was headed. She was a local, and he was not local at all. She was not going to leave her home, and the job she loved. He did not want to leave her, but his hold on being a local was dependent on Marcus. Therefore, they just left the issue to float out in the open like one of the many fishing boats off the coast.

It had been two days since William got the letter, and word was out that Marcus would be at the Blue Marlin that night. The usual frustration started to rear its ugly head when William had not heard from Marcus the day, he got the letter. However, William knew working for Marcus would be like that, and it was a small price to pay for a job in paradise. William took Maria down the stone street to the little bar with the blue marlin over it. Dinner did not start until at least after seven o'clock, and mostly after eight. It took William some getting used to, but now he was almost a local. William and Maria sat down and ordered two Moreti beers and started to talk. He did not know when, or if, Marcus would show. William had told Maria about the letter. They had an understanding that William could tell her about the various aspects of his workings with Marcus, but only on after work hours. Also, all of it was off the record. As a police officer she showed interest but cast a skeptical eye on the seriousness of it.

"I see these all the time," she said to William. "Many times it turns out nothing is behind it." William could not argue with her experience, but he still wanted to get the decision off his hands.

"So, what are you going to tell him?" Maria asked as the two walked back to a table. There were to waiting staff at the Blue Marlin. If you wanted something you had to get it yourself or sit at the bar.

"I don't know," William replied. "It's just a letter, and I don't know what to make out of it. Probably, it's just another one of Marcus little projects that is getting out of hand."

"It wouldn't be the first time," Maria replied as she took a drink from her beer.

Many of the locals know Marcus to be a crusader for some calling or idea. Given that he never had to worry about money, Marcus made his calling helping others in his own strange way. He had been around town for a while, so the locals took him in. He was very careful not to bring the American Bravo complex with him. Everyone liked him for that. Besides, he did not hurt his cause when he helps out many of the local businesses who were in need. Also, his gifts to the local church might have helped.

After an hour of sipping beers, and wondering if they had come from nothing, Marcus strolled through the door of a hangout that he considered a second home. He made his way past the bar, greeting a few familiar faces along the way. The bartender handed him a beer as he walked by. He saw William and Maria sitting in the back and made his way toward them.

"I see your still hanging out with this bum." He smiled at Maria. "I know his boss, and I hear he doesn't work very hard."

"I hear his boss is some lazy playboy who runs around with his boat all day," she replied. Marcus let out a laugh as he took the comment in stride. It was well known that once you get to know him, he can take about anything.

"So what's with this letter?" Marcus looked at William with an expression of curiosity. Without a word William handed the letter over to Marcus. He picked it up and studied it for a long while, much longer than it would take one to read that short of a letter. After setting it down on the table he picked up his beer and took a drink. No one spoke. Maria and William just looked at Marcus waiting for an explanation of a puzzle that had been bothering them for the past two days. Finally, Marcus spoke up.

"This complicates things." There was a period of silence.

"This complicates things," William said. "That is all. We get a letter like that, and it just complicates things. Could you tell me what things it complicates?" William regretted saying that as soon as the words came out of his mouth. He had prided himself on no even wanting to know what Marcus most of the time was up too. However, with this letter sitting in his lap for the last two days, his curiosity was getting the best of him.

"So now you want to know what is going on," Marcus said with a smile. "I don't know if I want to tell you." He let the words sit for a moment while he took another drink of his beer. Each of them knew damn well that Marcus would love to drag William along on whatever crazy ride this was. Marcus had respected William's request to be kept out of things.

"You know what I mean," William replied. "I don't want to be drug into whatever it is that is going on over there, but you told me to tell you about anything that looked important. This looked important. "Indeed, it is very important," Marcus said looking off at nothing. "It is very important." It did not look as though Marcus was going to get into much more detail as he sat in another silence that started to make William uneasy.

"If you are worried that I am going to get mad about being drug into something I don't want to know about, then just consider this your free pass," William said to get the conversation going. Marcus scratched the back of his head as though to indicate he did not know where to start.

"To tell you the truth I don't know much about what is going on over there," he said. "The only thing I did was send a little money to a friend who I thought could use it. I tend to do that sometimes." The last part gave William the idea that Marcus may be trying to put him in his place. Even so he pressed on.

"Who is Chris, where is this island, and who is the Leopard?"

"You know who Chris is, a map will show you where the island is, and I don't have the slightest idea who the Leopard is," Marcus said this with a hint of wonder as he finished his beer. William looked at him waiting for more of an answer.

"You give me too much credit," William replied. "I don't know who Chris is, and I couldn't find it on a map,"

"You must have the wrong map," Marcus said with a laugh. "Chris Lewis from Indiana."

Now that was a name William had heard before. Chris had been a fraternity brother in Sigma Alpha Epsilon at the University of Evansville. They did not know each other until college but had grown up only 20 miles apart. William wondered what the hell Chris had to do with anything Marcus had brewing.

"Let me tell you a little story." Marcus stood to round up three more beers. "It won't take long."

Marcus started into how he got a letter from an old Fraternity brother in Central America. A few years ago Marcus was living his ex-patriot life in Italy when he received a letter from Chris wondering how he was doing. A short letter exchange took place for a few weeks. Finally, Chris came around and asked for some money. Marcus was used to it, so it did not put him off. He always wanted to know why, and if the cause was good enough, he was happy to do it. Chris replied that he would like to study a bit in Central America and was a little short on funds. He had some money, but not enough to cover it. Marcus was fine with sending enough over to get him by.

"You know it doesn't really bother me when old friends come by and ask for something," he said looking at William. "Sometimes I even like it." Given his present living situation, William did not have much of a reply.

"I only got a couple of letters," Marcus said to them. "I didn't think much of it." He told them that he did not know why Chris needed the money, or how he was using it. He sent it out, but only got a small thank you note. However, it had been a while since he had heard from him. He knew that he had been going back and forth to Central America but was not sure why. Now a letter shows up from him in trouble in the very area Marcus thought he would be. Marcus did not have any advance warning about trouble. Chris had never mentioned anything about being in trouble, or that he would be doing anything that would get him into trouble.

"That's the thing," Marcus said with a puzzled look on his face. "I don't know where this is coming from."

"What do we do?" William asked.

"I don't know," Marcus replied. It was one of the few times William saw that Marcus did not know what to do when comforted with a problem. He was the one person that people usually went to when they had a problem, which explained Chris's letter, because he seemed to always know what to do.

The trio sat at the table for a few minutes with few words between them. Maria started to tell the boys a few bits about what had been happening around town. It was always good to hear the inside story about the real goings on. However, it was just filler to pass the time until someone came up with an idea of what to do. After about 15 minutes the conversation started to get stale. William and Maria could tell that it was weighing on Marcus.

"I think I am going to have to go over there," Marcus said as he looked down at the table.

"You are going to have to go where?" Asked Maria.

"I've got to go get him."

"Get him?" William exclaimed. "What do you mean go get him?"

"Who knows what is going on down there, he could be in real trouble," Marcus replied. "He sent me the letter. If I do not go, and something happens to him, how do you think I would feel?"

"You don't have to go racing around the world trying to bale people out of their problems," William said. "Just because you have money doesn't mean everyone is entitled to it." That was the main problem in Marcus' life. He had the means to help people, and sometimes they made him feel bad if he did not do it. He never had to work a day in his life. The trust fund made sure of that. However, he carried around a guilt complex that was easily exploited. If someone asked for money or help, he felt it his obligation to provide. That is why William had a nice place to stay and a part-time job.

"He is a friend and a Fraternity brother," Marcus replied with just hint of harshness in his voice.

"I know he is."

"Then why all the questions?"

"I am just wondering why you would think it necessary to go halfway around the world to check in on an old friend when you don't even know what it wrong," William said. Marcus paused for a moment and then a sly smile started to show.

"Because it would be an adventure." With that he finished his beer and sat back with his arms crossed and looked at William. The decision had been made, and there was nothing either of them could do about it. Once his mind was made up the deed was done. Besides, anything that had a bit of adventure to it was enough to get Marcus interested.

"Where do we start?" William conceded

"We?" Marcus asked.

"Yes we," William said. "I'm not letting you go out there alone. Besides, I have never been to Central America." Marcus was beaming knowing that his friend would come along. Maria smiled, and shook her head knowing that her boyfriend and his best friend were going off on a schoolboy adventure. For all his talk about just wanting to sit by the seaside she knew William really wanted to get out into the world and look around. She would have to live with that.

"Where do we start?" William asked.

"We need someone who has been there and speaks Spanish," Marcus replied. "No one from around here. We will have to go outside of Italy in case it is something that we don't want others to know." William thought for a second and a name from the past came in mind.

"What about Regis?" William asked Marcus.

"You mean Regis, like in the Regis from California?" Marcus said raising one eyebrow.

"I know he spent time wondering around Central America. He has spoken Spanish all of his life, and we know him from School," William replied. "That seems to be all we need in this little trip." Marcus set down his beer and shrugged.

"Then he is our man," Marcus said as he slapped the table. "Let's get him and get to the tropics."

"There is only one problem," William said.

"What's that?"

William was going to state a fact that he knew Marcus did not want to hear. Marcus had left the US a few years ago, and to William's knowledge rarely if ever returned. At no time did William remember Marcus telling him he wanted to go back. There had been trouble with family. William guessed it was either about money or lifestyle. Either way it was none of his business. Nothing else seemed to pull him back to his home country.

"We're going to have to go back to the States."

CHAPTER 6

Going back to the States was not something that Marcus took lightly. Since leaving years ago he went back rarely. He had made his life as an ex-pat and intended to keep it that way. Every once and a while he would go back and visit family. Each time he came back vowing it was the last time. There had been a few times that he had certain business dealings that needed to be attended to, but for the most part he kept himself away. There was just something about being back that he could not take for awfully long. Maybe it was the stuffy upper-class money that the rest of his family loved. A little bit of it was the omnipresent culture of stuff that surrounds every American no matter where they go. Each time he went he swore that he never wanted to go back. However, now his hand seemed to be forced.

Marcus wanted to go with people he trusted. Not that the people he trusted were necessarily the best people for the job. However, if that is what he wanted to do, then that is what he did. This trip would be no different. Strangely, in order to get to Costa Rica, and find the root of the problem with Chris, the two ex-pats would have to navigate through the streets of a newly rebuilt major American city. William was surprised by the contacts Marcus had kept. People that he had only known for a few months, or maybe a couple of years, were just a phone call away.

William only knew a few people that would recognize his voice if he called, and most of them were family. Now it was time to place one of those calls and see if another old friend would come along.

Regis had been a fraternity brother of William's for a couple of years before he ran back to California to start a business making everything out of hemp. A good guy, with a little bit too much of a love of Hemp and all of its uses. He was rumored to have mailed pot from California to Indiana through the US Mail without getting caught. He went out, and never came back. As with most of the guys that left, William heard bits and pieces of them from time to time. The last that he heard Regis was trying to make it in New Orleans. Through his sources Marcus had heard the same, and for unknown reasons decided to keep in touch. Regis had spent a few summers backpacking through Central America during college. He spoke fluent Spanish and was easy going without a need for much to get by on. Now it was going to be a party of three.

William was the one to get things together. Marcus had an idea of how to get a hold of Regis. Of course, it was not by cell phone or e-mail or something that could be confirmed. It was just the age-old custom of sending a letter out and hoping it got there before they did. William resisted the temptation to do it another way. He knew that if he deviated from Marcus' system, it would not be pretty. So he sent out the letter to Regis in New Orleans and made plans to fly the both of them out of Italy and into the United States. Marcus wanted to leave even before he heard back from Regis.

"How will we know that he even got the letter?" William asked.

"He will," Marcus replied. "Ye of little faith."

William hated when he said that. Marcus did not mind throwing caution to the wind. They would just fly out there and see what happened. After a year of being gone, and far away from the legal career he had planned for, William was heading back to the States. Fatefully, it was only a brief stopover.

Of course William wondered what in the hell he was supposed to take with him. They were going to a Central American country from an unknown period of time. He was sure that lugging around a huge suitcase was not going to work. William had always been an easy traveler, so he grabbed his backpack out of the closet, and filled it. Once nothing more could fit, he stopped. He did not have the slightest idea what Marcus would want to bring.

"We are going to the tropics." Then, William asked him, "So, what are you going to bring?"

"Just some light clothing," Marcus replied. "Casual, not something that will stick out."

"We will be a couple of Americans running around a Central American country looking for a friend that could be dead or in jail. How will we not stand out?" Marcus smiled at William knowing that he was right. Usually, Marcus had control of a situation. However, this time William could tell he was a bit out of his element. The one thing he could not tell is whether he was enjoying it or not.

Within two days the boys were ready to head back to the United States. It is wonderful what a bank account full of money can do for one's travels. Early on Marcus had given William the power to access all of his accounts, and his credit cards. However, William was still uneasy to do anything without going through Marcus first. William got permission from Marcus to find the first two tickets to New Orleans and buy them. When William saw the cost, he stopped for a brief moment. It was a sum that he would never be able to just fork over for a couple of plane tickets. He checked with Marcus one more time.

"Just buy them," he said after a short glance at the price. William took Marcus' credit card and charged them. He printed out the boarding passes and looked at the train schedule to Turin. They would leave in the morning.

They headed down to the train station to take the morning train to Turin. From there they would fly to London's Gatwick airport, and then on an overnight back to the United States. In all it would be a long couple of days for the two travelers. They had not spoken much about what they were going to do when they got there. Probably, because neither of them knew what was going to happen when they arrived. William was still unsure about how they would find Regis.

"How will we know that Regis knows we're coming?" Asked William.

"He'll be there," Marcus replied.

"Did you get a hold of him?"

"No, I just know that he will be there." That was it. There was no hint that Marcus thought things would go wrong. William on the other hand had a sneaky suspicion that everything could go wrong. As the train made its way slowly out of the station William knew that he had to put aside those feelings and go with his friend.

The train ride took them through North-Western Italy. They passed Pisa with its leaning tower. The train stopped for what seemed like hours in Genoa and got a look again at the Mediterranean Sea. Train travel in Italy was not a bad way to go. The train were comfortable, but nothing too fancy. They might not run on as tight a schedule as Germany, but it was close enough.

One could sit, and watch the country go by, or read a book. It was far better than sitting behind the wheel of a car for hours battling through traffic to get around.

The train made its way north to the City of Turin. A past host of the Winter Olympics, and home to the Shroud that proclaims to be the image of Jesus, Turin was a mix of the old and the new. Stepping out of their train William walked by a life-sized replica of the Shroud displayed in the station.

"Nothing like advertising the best you've got," William said to Marcus as they passed the Shroud.

From there they caught a taxi to take them to the airport. Marcus had noticed that William because more distracted the closer they got to Turin.

"Are you worried about what we will find in Costa Rica?" Marcus asked. Even though it was not warm on the train, Marcus could see that William was sweating.

"It's not that," replied William.

"Then what is it?"

William looked out the window at the planes flying out of the airport they were about to enter. His heart started to beat a bit faster, and his mouth became dry.

"Just don't like something but have to do it." Marcus and William had not traveled by plane together. They had a few road trips in the United States under their belt but had yet to fly together.

"What is it?"

"That," William said as he pointed toward a plane that just took off. Marcus did not realize that his friend was terrified of flying.

CHAPTER 7

The Colonel was eating breakfast and reading the morning paper. For the last year he had controlled what would go into the paper, so he did not read it for news. He read it to make sure that what he told the paper to say was in there, and that nothing else could sneak in. Once he was satisfied that the newspaper had done his bidding, he could turn his attention to other pressing matters. He had just finished a meeting with his closest advisors to feel out ways in which they could handle the growing problem of discontent.

The usual number of people had been picked up over the course of the last few days. Some of them would have to be held for a while, but most of them would get the message after a couple of days. They would be released back into the world, and most likely never heard from again. The idea was that if one were brought in for a few days in a dark and dirty cell, they would be less likely to speak out when they returned home.

With a handful of people going in and out during the month, the Colonel's plan was working. However, things had become complicated when he was told that an American had been taken in. All of his officers knew that foreigners were to be off limits for this sort of thing. Only in an extreme circumstance were a non-national to be held, and then it was only for a very short time. Now we had a foreign national in jail, and worst of all an American. He knew that the American's were the most likely to make noise, and noise is not what the Colonel wanted.

Even though he had a lot on his mind, the breakfast spread in front of him was not neglected. He had promised an answer to the American problem before lunch, and he had no idea what to do. The plan had been working perfectly so far. Bumps in the road were all a part of it, but this seemed more than just a bump. He knew that if word got out of his plans for the island he would be taken down. He had created a system that worked for an exceedingly small amount of people, with himself at the top. A plan was in place to make sure that he was taken care of for the rest of his life. Therefore, he was intent on letting nothing get that plan off track. That meant that he needed to take a look for himself. Normally, the Colonel did not like to see firsthand how his orders were being carried out. Even though he would talk a good deal about what a strong leader he was, in truth, he liked to leave the tough stuff to others. He liked most of all to bark orders at people and watched them get it done. He only got his hands dirty when absolutely necessary. However, in this case he was curious. He wondered why a 20 something American would come all this way to make trouble. It was time for the Colonel do get his hands dirty.

He finished up the last remaining food on the table and made his way to the door. A guard at the door snapped to attention as he passed.

"I need my car," he said. "I am going to check on things myself." The guard saluted like in the manner the Colonel had instructed him to do, not knowing in the least what the Colonel was taking about. The car was ordered to come around.

It was a strange order considering the close proximity the jail was to him at the moment. Nevertheless, the Colonel stood under the awning that shaded him from the ever-rising sun as a guard brought the car around for his two-minute drive. If he would have chosen to walk, he would have been there already, but dictators did not walk. It was about the show, and the Colonel knew it. He also liked the show as much as anyone.

A whole entourage of people went with him. Three carloads of guards, and assistants drove the short distance to the detention center. Once there the Colonel rolled out of his car to be followed by this gaggle of people into the building. Having fifteen people show up for a surprise inspection brought the unwanted attention of many people in the area. However, there was little that could be done to shield curious eyes away from the parade, so the Colonel just went inside.

There was not enough space in the detention center for the whole group, so many of them were stranded out in the waiting area with no air conditioning, and very little to do. A couple of guards went back through the metal door to the holding area. As he passed through looks of surprise crossed the faces of many in there. No one knew he was coming, and none of them had ever been this close to the Colonel. Quizzical looks were exchanged between the head of the center and the Captain of the guards who was on duty that day as the Colonel approach.

"It is very good to have you here sir," said the Captain "It is an unexpected surprise." The Colonel nodded to him, and never gave him another thought.

"I want to see the American," he demanded of no specific person. "I want to see him now." Immediately the guards started to wrangle keys from their pockets, and doors began to open.

The Colonel went back to the area where the inmates were kept. He passed rows of cells with curious looking persons peering out between the bars. He did not care who they were. Some of them were there because they were criminals in need of jail. Every time one of those was caught the Colonel made sure it was front page news. Several of them were for violent crime, but most were drugs. Nothing like a war on drugs to make the populous forget about a war on freedom. The guards led him pass all of the cells until he came to another metal door.

"Why did we pass all of the inmates?" the Colonel asked.

"The American is back here," replied the guard. "Captain wanted to keep him away from the others. He thought he might cause trouble."

The Colonel thought it was the right thing to do, but worried about holding a man that could not even be kept with the others.

He was led down a narrow hall that was lit by only two small lights dangling from the ceiling. The air was heavy and tough to breath. At the end of the hallway was a small cell containing one very ragged person. Chris sat in the corner of his cell staring down at the ground. When the Colonel approached him the prisoner barley lifted his head. People came in and out all of time, and Chris gave them little notice. However, when he looked up, he saw a man dressed in a military uniform looking down at him.

"Does he speak Spanish?" the Colonel asked the guard in a quiet voice.

"Yes," the guard replied.

"Good," yhe Colonel knew some English, but it was not particularly good. He was also smart enough to ask and make sure he knew whether Chris could understand what they were saying when he was around.

The guard unlocked the door, and the Colonel stepped inside the cell. Chris did not know who this man was, but he was obviously important. He had a better uniform than any of the other men that had come to see him, and more metals. He could not figure out how a man in Costa Rica could even earn a metal let alone many metals. The Colonel looked down at him with an expression of annoyance more than anger. Nothing was said for a few seconds as the men sized each other up.

"Why are you here?" asked the Colonel.

"You look like a person that should know," Chris replied.

The Colonel did not look amused. He took a step toward Chris.

"I know why you are here but was wondering if you know why you are here," he told Chris. "So, I will ask you again, why are you here?" Chris did not break eye contact and sat silent for a moment. He knew it probably would not do him any good to play games, so he decided to just talk.

"Some guys crashed a meeting I was attending," Chris replied. "They drug me out and put me in here." Of course, the Colonel knew this. It was just one of many meetings he had ordered broken up and had his police force make blanket arrests.

"No, I mean, why are you in my country?" The Colonel smiled as he said this and moved closer to Chris. Now he was nearly standing over Chris. Sitting at the feet of a man in a military uniform, Chris knew that he must watch what he said. The phrase of the question caught in Chris's mind. The way the man said "my country" was more of ownership than citizenship. The Colonel was trying to make him feel small, and it was working.

"I am just visiting," he replied.

"You are doing more than just visiting," the Colonel said staring down at Chris. "You are not just some tourists combing through the shops and restaurants." The Colonel peered down at him as he moved his face closer to Chris. "I know you are here for a reason, and I don't play games. You can tell me what is behind this, or you can stay here and think about it for a while."

Chris thought for a moment and said, "I guess I need a little time to think." He tried to sound brave.

The Colonel laughed "I guess you are the tough guy." The guards started to laugh with him. "We have had a lot of tough guys here. They don't seem that tough when I am done with them." With that, the Colonel turned and left the cell. The guard slammed the cell door closed with a loud bang. Chris sat there watching the Colonel walking away and wondering if he was ever going to get out of that cell.

CHAPTER 8

Riding in a plane had always been something William tried to avoid. One of the biggest worries of his travels to Europe was that he would have to take a plane to get there. At one point he had even contemplated taking a ship across the Atlantic. However, a cooler head had prevailed, and the ensuing seven-hour ride was tolerated. Now he faced that task again. The airport bar was the first place they went. Since they had over an hour to wait Marcus decided to feed William a few drinks to make the time pass. A few drinks turned into five drinks as William tried to dull the worry about his impending nine-hour flight to the States.

They were to fly into Louis Armstrong international airport in New Orleans. There they were to meet Regis in order to facilitate their entry into Latin America. William wondered whether Marcus was making some sort of arraignments without him. He did not understand how three people were supposed to just pop down to Central America to pick up a friend. How they would meet up with a guy they had not seen in years is something William just left up to fate.

William was never much of a drinker. In college he spent more time looking out for others who were drinking, than he did not drinking himself. Once he arrived in Italy, he easily embraced the culture of drinking socially. Sitting with a group of people for a long dinner, and having a few drinks was natural. Sure, one might have several drinks, but it was over the course of a few hours. Drinking in his adopted town was never with the intention of getting drunk. It was merely another facet of social interaction. If one happened to get drunk it was only a by-product. However, it seemed now that Marcus was intent on getting him drunk as quickly as possible. William did not mind as long as it helped him get through the flight.

Marcus only had one drink but kept handing William another. Things went downhill quickly at the fifth drink. William remembered getting up from the table and making his way toward the gate. Everything was moving in slow motion as Marcus sat him down in a seat in front of the gate. The fifth drink is what may have done it William thought. It was working amazingly fast now. This was not like going down to the Blue Marlin and having a few drinks with friends. Something was different about the way William felt.

The pretty lady with the microphone announced something that made everyone move toward the gate. William looked around, and people were moving in slow motion. Marcus grabbed both of their bags and started to move. So, William got up and followed Marcus. They handed their tickets to the lady and made their way down the long corridor towards the plane. William could feel his eyes getting heavier, and his vision getting narrower. All he knew was that he needed to make it to one of the seats on the plane.

At this point he did not even care which one. If they would have let him, he would have laid down, and fallen asleep right there. There was a line of people in front of him so his progress toward the plane slowed. He felt very tired, or very drunk.

He could not figure out which one it was. William knew that he had drank five beers pretty quickly but had not remember a time when the alcohol hit him this hard.

"I don't think I can handle that much beer anymore," William said to Marcus as he tried to keep everything in focus.

"Not feeling good?" Marcus said with a laugh. He did not seem too concerned with his friend's state of mind. "Don't worry, not too much further to go. Then you can have a nice nap on the plane until we get there."

"I don't know if I will make it to the plane," William said as his eyes started to close.

"Hang in there, buddy, we'll get you there."

Marcus put his arm around William and started to laugh at him. The other passengers were giving a few bad looks at the two Americans. Most of the Italians just chalked it up to another case of Americans behaving badly in Europe. Marcus did not care, and William was not able to understand much of anything at the time.

Finally, the two made it passed the doorway, and into the plane. Since it was to be an overnight flight, it was a big plane. There were seats on the side, and a five-seat wide row in the middle. Marcus and William had lucked out and gotten two seats on the outside by the wings. Marcus dropped William in the seat next to the window, with his eyes half open. His small carry-on bag was sitting in his lap. William closed his eyes and leaned his head back against the seat. Marcus took the bags and placed them under the seats in front of them. He buckled up William and sat down. Marcus took out an old baseball cap and put it on William's head. William grabbed the rim and pulled it down over his eyes. At least now no one will know how bad he felt.

"So, no first-class, Mr. Rich guy?" William asked practically drooling on the window at this point.

"I don't think you would quite fit in," Marcus replied. "Besides, you are always telling me that I have to watch what I spend."

"I didn't mean this time," William said.

"I will keep that in mind the next time we fly."

"There won't be a next time," William replied as Marcus settled into his seat as the final passengers made their way onto the plane.

"I think its nap time," William said as he passed out in his seat. Marcus got comfortable and began looking at the in-flight information sheet. A flight attendant approached him looking quizzically at his friend.

"Is your friend alright?" she asked.

"Yes, I think he will be just fine," Marcus replied.

"Is he feeling ill?" she asked, hoping that everyone did not have to be stuck in an enclosed space for nine hours with a contagious disease.

"No, he just needed a little help getting through the long flight." With that he held up a bottle of sleeping pills that he had in his pocket. Marcus thought that five beers might not do it, so he gave the last one a little help. The flight attendant took one look at the bottle and rolled her eyes. She gave a quick look over to a sleeping William and left it at that. The plane taxied down the runway with Marcus checking on the in-flight movie, and William sound asleep never knowing that he was already airborne. Marcus had giving him enough pills to last almost the whole flight.

CHAPTER 9

The sound of a crowd cheering is all he needed to brighten up his day. This is what he lived for. The small plaza was filled to capacity to hear the speech. Of course, it helped that the government gave most of the people the day off of work and handed out free food and drinks in the plaza. As far back as ancient Rome, the ruling class would use the bait of free entertainment, and refreshments, to gain a large crowd. It worked then, and it still worked on his island.

The Colonel had been prepping for this all week. He would sit in his office surrounded by aides, and try out new phrases, and promises, to see their effect. Most of the time those around him just nodded and told him everything he said was wonderful. After everyone had left, and he was alone in his room, the Colonel would stand in front of his mirror and practice. He would practice his facial expressions, and movements. He looked at his life as a part in a play. His speech would be just around two hours long. Much shorter that some of his famous four-hour speeches that he had been known to give. The weather was going to be hot, and he did not want to have to provide for everyone the entire day.

For days, the Colonel had poured over different versions of his speech. He needed to warn the people about outside agitators who were causing trouble on their beloved island. They needed to be told about criminal elements in their mist that threaten their way of life, and their families. The Colonel needed them to know that he was their protector, and that he would be there to look out for them. Most of all he needed them to know that in order to do this he would need their help. The enemy could be the man down the street. It could be their neighbor, or it could even be their friend. He needed them to become the State and help seek out those who would cause trouble. Only when they trusted in him to bring them their deliverance would the island be saved. It was a masterpiece in propaganda, and he loved it like a child.

As the time for the speech grew near, he allowed the crowd to wait. He wanted to build the anticipation to maximum effect. As he stepped out on the balcony a roar went up from the crowd. The people loved the spectacle and wanted to feel as though they were a part of something bigger than themselves. The Colonel strode out in front of the mass of people and waved the short wave of a dictator. He was wearing his favorite uniform. The sheer weight of it would stress most men, but he bore it well. There were enough medals on it to kill at least three metal detectors, and the glare could burn a hole through lead. The sun shone down on him high above his people. Without hesitation he launched into his speech.

"Today we stand together," he stated. "We face an enemy from within." With that the crowd cheered. Not everyone could hear what he was saying, but when some started to cheer the others joined in.

"From within our own island we are facing those who want to bring crime and chaos to our homes. They want to disrupt our peaceful existence and drive us from our prosperity. They want to take from us what we have earned." This was news to almost all who heard it. Most of the people of the island did not know they were in so much trouble. The peaceful existence had not been disrupted for many of the people on the island. Their lives had gone on, for the most part, like it had for years. Only a small portion of the people who lived in the city had been affected. However, it was not from anyone except the government, and their agents.

"Now there is a new threat." The Colonel paused to let this news take effect. Not only had there been numerous criminal elements out there that the people did not know about, but now there was to be a new one. The crowd awaited news of the next coming disaster.

"We have just learned that this criminal element has reached a new level," the Colonel said. "Now outside influences have come to our island to cause more trouble." The words outside influence did not go over well with the crowd. Hisses and boos started to echo up to the balcony. The Colonel knew he had hit the note he was looking for. Crime from within was unsettling, but something most expected to tolerate. However, disaster from the outside was in all ways unacceptable.

"They have come to our country and are trying to influence our way of life. They are trying to take away our culture, and attack how we live. These foreigners are coming into our towns, and our villages, and destroying our way of life." This was too much for the crowd to bear. Howls and shouts drown out anything the Colonel was trying to say. That is what the Colonel wanted from them. He stood over them listening to their cries. He knew it was time to ask them to give him the power that he wanted.

"I ask for my people to listen," he told them as they started to quiet down. "I am here to protect you. I vow to spend my days making sure all of these people are brought to justice." Of course, the Colonel never actually said who these people were, or what they were doing. Not to mention that there was never a discussion of what justice they were to be brought to. Nevertheless, the crowd loved it. With the day off of work, a bite to eat, and the knowledge that their leader was going to save them, the people were ready to give up their freedom.

"The people have spoken," he continued. "They have said that we will not stand for this. Those who oppose us will be brought to jail, and they will never again see the chance to harm us again." The crowd then gave its loudest cheer. The Colonel basked in its glory and waved to the crowd. For a moment he stood there for all to see. The people were his, and he knew that there would be little opposition.

"I think we will have what we want now," the Colonel said to those around him. "There will be little to stop us now." The crowd was still cheering as he held up his hand for silence.

"I have a plan to lead us into the future." The crowd also loved that. "Let me tell you how it will begin." With that the Colonel launched into an hours-long, rambling lecture that lead nowhere and did not touch on how things could be better in the future. However, very few seemed to care. The Colonel was right. If he talked long enough people would forget that nothing was really said.

The crowd grew tired from standing in the heat. Just when they could not take much more, the Colonel concluded his remarks. The crown gave up one last cheer. This one much less energetic than the previous ones and started to leave the square.

The Colonel took out a small cloth and wiped his head. He headed back into the building and headed to his office.

Sitting in his chair with the air conditioning working at maximum power, the Colonel had unbuttoned his uniform to cool off. His advisors were scattered around the room all trying to recover after hours standing under the sun.

"Now I need to finish what we have started," the Colonel told his chief of police. "The people are willing to go all of the way with me on this. It is your job to find out who is against us."

"And then what?" the Chief asked.

"You bring them to me."

CHAPTER 10

For Marcus, the plane ride was fairly uneventful. He watched a not all together bad movie and had really bad airline food. His friend slept somewhat peacefully next to him as they glided along the air at 500 mile per hour. Marcus spent much of the time thinking about what they would have to do once they got to Costa Rica. He was fairly certain that things would work out in the States. They would find Regis, even if he did not show up at the airport.

Money goes a long way in the States, and that was something Marcus had a lot of. However, things would be different down in the Banana Republics. The biggest problem that Marcus kept running into was that they did not know what trouble was waiting for them. Every now and then Marcus would secretly hope that they would go down there and find Chris saying that it was all just a big misunderstanding. They would hang out, have some drinks, and go home with another funny story to tell.

It had been around six hours since take off, and only then had William started to stir. He would open his eyes for a couple of seconds, and then close them again for a minute.

"How long have I been on this plane?" William asked.

"We are over halfway there," Marcus replied. "How do you feel?"

"Swung at and missed, but shit on and hit," William said. "Can I get something to drink?" Marcus flagged down the flight attendant and asked for a bottle of water.

"O.K. what the hell went on back there?" William asked now realizing that a few beers, and that much sleep, did not add up.

"I gave you a little help to get on the plane," Marcus said with a smile. "Relax we will be back home in a couple of hours."

"That is part of the reason I can't relax," William replied.

The flight attendant came with the water, and Marcus and William started to talk about what to do once they got to the States. Both decided that they did not need to spend much time there. All of them had passports to get to Costa Rica. All they needed to do was pick up Regis and make their way down to San Jose on the first available flight. Marcus would handle the logistics, and the money. William seemed to be along for the ride. Neither of them wanted to spend much time in New Orleans. Deep inside both of them worried that something serious was going on with Chris, and that they should get down there to find out as soon as possible.

Both of them seemed a bit nervous as the plane descended into Louis Armstrong International Airport. Marcus wondered what to do next. William worried about the plane landing. He wondered if Marcus could just knock him out again but realized that he needed to be clear headed when they got to town. However, everything went as planned and the plane touched down in their home country. They grabbed their belongings and headed off the plane.

"It's kind of strange to be back, isn't it?" William said.

"You said it," Marcus replied. They looked around at the airport like they had not seen America in 30 years.

"Not as different as I thought it would be," Marcus said.

"Just wait."

Since they were American it was not too hard to clear customs. Most of the people were from other countries, and the line for citizens was short. They were done in under a half an hour, which is good for that sort of thing. Now they faced their first real problem. They needed to find Regis.

"How are we going to find him?" Asked William.

"I told him about when we were going to arrive," Marcus replied. "We are just about on time, so I hope he is waiting with a little sign with our names on it." With that Marcus smiled and headed toward the exit to the arrival pick up area. William picked up his bag and followed. He looked around at his homecoming and felt a bit out of place. One could tell right away that the pace of life was a bit faster here than in Sevena. The people were also much bigger, and the food looked a lot worse. However, it was a consolation that everything was written in English. For William, even though he tried hard, it was tough to master Italian.

Marcus walked through the automatic doors that lead to the pick-up area for arriving flights. There was no Regis to be found. William walked up to where he was standing and sat down his bag.

"What do we do now?"

"I guess we wait," Marcus said as he walked to the side and sat down. "He'll be here." William looked around for a minute and tried to remember what Regis looked like. It had been a few years since he had seen him but thought that he would be able to recognize the face. Surely, they had not changed that much in a couple of years.

So, the two sat there and watched the traffic go by. The heat was starting to rise and made everything sticky. There was an African American traffic cop trying to organize the chaos in the road the best he could. Waving cars here and there with a flourish that made it look like he was dancing to music. Then a car came creeping right up next to him, and almost bumped him.

"Whoa…back it up, baby!" he said, laughing at the driver and jumping out of the way. It sounded like this was not his first day on the job.

Marcus and William sat on the curb waiting for Regis to show up. They had nowhere to go and did not know what type of car to look for. All they could do was sit there and wait. After a few minutes William got up and stretched his legs.

"I am going for a walk," he said.

"Don't go far," Marcus replied. William picked up his bag and started to walk down the sidewalk. After making it about twenty yards he saw a young man dressed in khaki pants and a button-down blue shirt. He looked lost, and he looked familiar.

"That has to be him," William said. He walked a little closer to the man standing on the sidewalk looking around trying to find two guys he had not seen in a few years. As William looked at him, he could tell that it was Regis. Not much had changed in the face, but the wardrobe was something that he did not expect.

"It's about time," William yelled from about 20 feet. "We were starting to wonder about you."

Regis turned and looked at William. A big smiled came across his face.

"It's you!" He exclaimed. "I can't believe you are standing here." The two shock hands as William guided Regis over to where Marcus was sitting. There was another warm welcome when Regis and Marcus met. Although tired Marcus, and William, were glad to have finally met up with Regis. Both were ready to get a shower, and maybe some food.

The three reunited friends walked back to where Regis parked the car. He had obviously been looking for quite some time because it took a while to find the car. William hopped in the back while Marcus rode shotgun. They exited the airport and made their way to Reverend Richard Wilson Dr.

"I'll take you the scenic route," Regis said as he turned the car east along the Mississippi River. It soon turned into the Jefferson Highway running along the river toward downtown. William had never seen New Orleans before. Seeing new places had always excited him. The excitement was dimmed a bit this time given that he was travel worn, and still worried about Chris. William looked out his window, and watched the city start to go by. Even with hours of napping William was a bit tired. There had been a huge change in time as they traveled, and his body was thinking it was much later than the clock was showing. William closed his eyes, and tried to imagine being back by the sea, and Maria. He was concerned about Chris and wanted to get him out of whatever it was that he was in, but he also wanted to get back home as quick as he could to Maria. The Highway turned into South Carrollton Ave. Soon they again turned East on Green Street to Regis' house. It was a nice single-story home. A lot nicer than William thought Regis would have at this time.

"Nice house," William said not wanting to know how Regis could afford it.

"Thanks, not a bad place to live," replied Regis. He went on to say that he was only a couple of blocks away from Tulane University, and Audubon Park. They went up the steps and Regis unlocked the door.

"Mi casa es su casa," he said. William set down his bag and took a look around. The house was another surprise. It was small, but well kept. Much different than anything William remember about Regis' housekeeping in college. After his short tour, William came back into the room and saw Marcus and Regis on the couch talking.

"So, what do we do from here?" he asked.

"I think we should take the night off and see some of the town," said Marcus. William was a bit stunned. He was ready to just hang around the house and talk about how to get down to Costa Rica, and then maybe grab a bite to eat.

"I thought we were going to hang low, and take it easy?" Said William. "Why the change in plans?"

"We have never been here before, and Regis said he wanted us to see the French Quarter," Marcus replied. "Only for a while, then we will come back and get working." Marcus actually looked like he wanted to go, and Regis looked like a dog getting a treat for good behavior. William did not want to crash the party so he said that would be fine.

"How are we going to get there, and when are we going," William said sounding defeated.

"The St. Charles Streetcar, and in about 20 minutes," replied Regis.

William did not have much time to get his bearings. Both Marcus and Regis seemed like they wanted to leave and have a night on the town. All he wanted to do was lay down and take a nap. However, like any other twenty something male, he sucked it up and went out with his friends. With a quick wash of his face and hands he changed clothes and was at the door in fifteen minutes. He did not care what he looked like since he already had a beautiful girlfriend back home. That made it easier to get ready and head out.

The three walked a few blocks south through the campus, and found the streetcar stop. It was early in the evening and the students from Tulane and Loyola University were milling about. It had only been a few years since his days in college, but he could already feel the wide gulf between him and the students he watched.

"The car should be here in a couple of minutes," Regis said. "It's only a couple of bucks for the ride into the Quarter." So, they waited until the St. Charles Ave. Streetcar pulled up. They hopped on and William sat down on one of the wooden seats in the middle of what looked like a tourist convention.

"Most of the riders are sightseeing," Regis told him. "But it's a good and cheap way to get downtown." The streetcar windows were open to the evening air. After being on a plane for most of the last day it was a welcome change. The car made its way passed nice Victorian Mansions from the Old South. Most of the neighborhoods were nice as they made the way toward the French Quarter. William was half paying attention to what was going by. He was finding it hard to keep only one thought in his mind. Marcus and Regis sat in the row across from him discussing what to do when they got out of the States. William did not seem too concerned to join the conversation. He just wanted to sit and let his mind wander.

As they got closer to the French Quarter the city sprang up around them. The streetcar made its way through the business district down Carondele Street. The street seemed closed in as they traveled down the road. Cars were trying to pass through the tight street, and people seemed to be everywhere. The sun had crossed the horizon, and yet the New Orleans air was still hot and sticky. They clacked down the track until the car pulled up to Canal Street on the edge of the French Quarter. Across the Street lay the French Quarter where Carondele Street turned into the much more famous Bourbon Street. Throngs of people walked up and down Canal Street, jumping in and out of traffic as they went. The three of them got off the streetcar and started to walk to the Quarter.

"This doesn't look like much," said William

"We're not quite there yet," Regis replied. They walked down Canal Street toward the river. The air was still heavy, but with no sun the shadows gave a hint of coolness to the new evening. The three made their way down past Chartres Street and Hotels Charging a premium to be within staggering distance from the action. The cut through Badine Street past the parking lots and crossed the trolley tracks toward Woldenburg Park. The Mississippi River slowly crept toward the Gulf of Mexico just in front of them. William had seen the river many times, but all of them were from up North. The river was much wider here in the south before it ended its run into the sea.

There were families out for an evening stroll, and several homeless people laid out on tattered blankets with change jags out for help. William walked along a little bit behind Marcus and Regis. They had been absorbed in some sort of conversation that he was not too terribly interested in being a part of.

"Are you staying with us?" Marcus turned around and asked.

"Just taking it in," William replied. After hearing about the French Quarter, he wanted to see what everyone was talking about. They made a left on St. Peters Street toward Decatur. Regis stopped them at the corner.

"Here we are," Regis said, "Jackson Square." As they came about what looked like a city park was in front of them. At its back was a big Catholic Church. They crossed Decatur Street, and walked down the pedestrian only walkway beside the park. There were artist and tarot card readers set up in makeshift spots to cater to the tourists.

"This is amazing," William told Regis. People were everywhere. He stopped in front of an artist in the middle of painting. It was a picture of the Cathedral in dark blues and gray.

"There is some real talent here, if you stop and look close enough," Regis said as he walked up beside him. "A little bit of con artists too." Marcus had walked through a gate into the park going toward a statue of Andrew Jackson, the namesake of the park. William kept walking until he came to the front of the church. As sort of a buffet Catholic, he stood in front of the St. Louis Cathedral, and saw that he was surrounded by streets of Saints Peter and Ann on both sides. He looked around to see crowds of people moving along the streets. Along with the artists that had set up shop on the sidewalks, street performers had staked out claims on good perches for passerby dollar collections. This was far away from the sleepy Italian village that he had adopted, and seemed almost foreign to the small-town Indiana he grew up in.

"Let's get a drink, and maybe something to eat," Marcus suggested as he and Regis joined William, obviously enjoying the surroundings.

"Try a hand grenade," Regis said.

"What the hell is that?" William asked.

"Trust me. You'll like it." With that they walked up St. Ann Street past Royal and turned left on Bourbon Street. This was the main drag of the French Quarter, and where most of the action seemed to be. It was a bit crowed, and William was starting to feel this might not be the place for him. As they stood on the corner William overheard a local talking to a man and woman in their 50's dressed in flower print shirts.

"If I guess where you got your shoes, you owe me twenty dollars," said the local man. "I tell you where you got yo shoes."

"No way you can guess, but I will take your bet," replied the flower printed tourist.

"You got your shoes right here on Bourbon Street," said the local. "They are right here on the sidewalk."

The tourist tilted his head and looked at his wife. They started to walk away, but the local would not have any of it.

"Hey, I did my part where the twenty dollars?" Not wanting any more part of this scam and trying to just get out of there the man held out a twenty as he walked away. *Yet another day's work,* William thought.

"This is crowded," William said.

"This is nothing," Regis replied. "This is an off night. You should see it in February. Girl hanging out of balconies people everywhere. It's one of the craziest things I've seen." As they walked down Bourbon Street it did not seem like what William had heard about. He had been in the French Quarter for almost 20 minutes and not one girl had taken her shirt off. Not that he really wanted to get mixed up in that.

"You probably won't see that on a night like tonight," Regis said. "They save that for Marti Gras."

That was OK for William, he had a girlfriend at home.

They stopped at the Tropical Isle and Regis bought three Hand Grenades. They came in plastic cups that stated they were the strongest drink in New Orleans.

"What's in it?" Marcus asked.

"Don't know," Regis replied as he eyed some College girls who were stumbling down the street. The streets were busy, but not overcrowded. The sun had set, and the cool evening air was starting to take hold. The three walked down Bourbon Street taking in the sights. It did not take long for each of them to finish their drinks and start the search for a new one.

They stopped at the Bourbon Street Blues Company and headed to the bar. There was a stage in the front where a band had started to set up their gear. The bar was toward the back, and Marcus ordered three Long Island Iced Teas.

"What's with the Iced Teas?" William asked

"Bartender said it was a special," Marcus replied as he tasted his drink. William wanted to make fun of the rich guy who ordered drink specials but thought better of it. Given that it felt better outside than inside they headed out into the evening air.

"So how are we going to do this?" Regis asked as the three stood on the sidewalk watching the people go by.

"Do you mean, do we have a plan?" Marcus replied.

"Something like that."

"We don't." With that Regis looked at Marcus and then at William. Neither of them had a plan as of what to do next other than head down to Costa Rica and find out what was going on.

"So, are we just going to go down there and try and find out what the hell is going on?" Regis asked.

William and Marcus looked at each other and nodded.

"Yeah, that's about it," William said. Regis looked a bit worried and finished up his drink. As they walked down by Music Legends Park, and turned north on Bienville, they found a little shop selling Po Boy sandwiches. The guys found a table and sat down. They ordered Po Boys and some Dixie beers. Now they finally had time to start and think about what to do when they got there.

As they talked a plan of sorts came about. They would fly out of New Orleans as soon as they could get a flight into Costa Rica. Marcus would take care of that. They would make their way to the coast and find a hotel. There they would make their way over to the island and check things out. No one would pay them much attention. Three Americans down on a Holiday happened all the time there. They would try and look like regular tourists and find out as much as possible. The one thing none of them could figure out was the Leopard. Marcus had asked Regis if he remembered anything about Chris that had anything to do with a Leopard. Regis had no idea, but in his defense, it was hard for him to remember much of anything. They agreed that it was probably something Chris came across down there, and it would be easier to figure out when they got there.

After they had emptied a few beers the talked strayed away from finding Chris, and more about the fun times they had in college. It was not hard to waste an hour or two sitting at a table talking with old friends over beers. Finally, after about five rounds the boys got up and started back into the streets. More and more people had come out for the night, and the streets were filled with locals looking at tourists, with tourists looking at street performers, and pickpockets looking at tourists looking at street performers.

They made their way back down to Bourbon Street. This time it took a bit longer given they were around six or seven drinks deep. William was holding his own since he had a bit to eat, but he was clearly feeling the effects. Just off Bienville Street they spotted the Old Absinthe House. The doors were open, and it seemed an inviting place to sit down.

"So, William," Regis asked as they sat down, "how did you get over there with Marcus?"

"Good question," William replied. "Have a shot, and I'll tell you."

The shots went down, and William started to tell his story. Even Marcus was amused in getting details that he may not have heard before. William started telling them about how he had been sitting in the room at the Bar Examination in downtown Indianapolis. He had already been through around a day and half of testing. He had a little bit left to go, and he just sat there and looked around.

At that moment, all he wanted to do was get out of there. He scribbled some answers down on the paper in front of him, and got up to turn them in. Only one person had finished before him, but he did not care. He burst through the doors of the convention center where the test was taking place into the hot summer air of central Indiana in August. He did not want anything at all to do with the law at that point and could frankly care less if he passed the test. He went home and sat in the backyard of his parent's house thinking about what to do next.

Since he had lived at home, he had saved up a little money. He knew he had to get out. Later that night he told his parents that he needed some time away after Law School and was going for a break. They were used to him taking off on his own so there were few questions. The next day he grabbed a bag of stuff and headed to the airport. He caught a flight to New York and stayed at a hotel just a block north of the Empire State Building. Standing in front of that massive tower of human engineering he thought up a plan. He would fly to Italy and find an old friend.

"That is what I did," William said proudly with a little slur in his speech.

"Indeed, it is," Marcus replied as they raised their glasses for a toast.

They had found their groove and staggered from one drinking hole to the next as the night carried on. Marcus was holding his own, William was hanging on, and Regis was three sheets to the wind. They made their way to the corner of St. Peter Street and Bourbon when they decided they needed a place to sit down. It was getting late, and they needed to figure out how to get home.

They stepped into Pat O'Brien's and Marcus led Regis to the Courtyard in the middle of the place to find a seat. William spotted a bar near the entrance and walked up and sat down. Even though there was no reason to order even one more drink, William made his best attempt to order another. All he got out was a grunt, and a hand gesture to the patron next to him that had ordered a beer. William held up two fingers and put money on the bar. The bartender sat down two Budweiser and scooped up the money laughing at William. Grabbing the beers William headed into the Courtyard to find his friends.

He found them sitting at a table with a couple of bowls of popcorn in front of them.

"What's that?" William asked.

"Popcorn"

"I know its popcorn. Where did you get it?"

"Some lady just came around and gave us some popcorn," Marcus said. "I thought it might help sober Regis up." William looked over and saw Regis face down in a bowl of popcorn eating it without hands."

"I don't think he is doing too well," William said.

"At least he is eating," Marcus replied. William handed him a beer and sat down. Marcus looked at the beer as though it was a ticking time bomb. William took one drink of his and winced. Both knew there was no need for anymore. Regis stopped eating his popcorn and stared off into the distance.

"You OK man?" Marcus slurred. There was no response.

"I think it's time to get out of here," William said. Marcus agreed, and they grabbed their quiet, intoxicated friend and made their way to the door. It had gotten late, and the streets were starting to clear. Regis was having trouble walking now, and Marcus and William had to help him down the street.

"How do we get home Regis?" Marcus would ask as they walked down the street. Regis would only mumble something and then stop. All of a sudden Regis shot straight up and did not look good. The guys let go and Regis staggered over to the sidewalk and proceeding to throw up what had to have been the largest pile of popcorn William had ever seen.

"How much did he have?" William asked.

"Obviously, too much," Marcus replied.

Once the retching was over William and Marcus grabbed him again and started to walk. They looked quiet out of place. They got looks from people who passed them, most shaking their heads.

"You better get home, you people got shot around here looking like that!" a homeless man yelled at the three.

"I'll get a gun and shot," Regis mumbled to himself.

"Time to get the hell out of here," Marcus said as they turned toward Jackson Square. They made it down St. Peters Street to Decatur and stopped.

"We'll just get a taxi and get back to his house," Marcus said. "Regis how do we get to your house?" Marcus asked to the barely conscious Regis.

"My house," was his only reply.

"We'll be sleeping in a car if you don't help us," William said starting to get a bit mad.

"No sleep car...sleep car bad," Regis said.

Marcus flagged down a taxi and asked him if he could take them to the Tulane campus. The driver said that was fine, and they started to get in.

"No way, not that guy," the driver said. "He is not puking in my cab."

"I think he is OK," William said in a blatant lie.

"No way." The guys could not leave him there, and they did not have any other way to get back. So they asked the driver if there was any way he would let him in the car. The driver went to the trunk and pulled out a black plastic garbage bag.

"Here put this over him." They got in the taxi and sat Regis in between them with a garbage bag over his head. Soon Regis was slumped over, and the bag had gone completely over his head, and his shoulders.

"Don't let him suffocate," William said.

"He is still breathing," Marcus replied. The only sound coming from Regis was a random "no sleep car…sleep car bad. Driving along with what looked like a dead body in the backseat with them William was very tired. They had no idea how to get into Regis' house, but at least they would be somewhere safe.

The taxi pulled up to the Campus of Tulane and dropped them off. William and Marcus hauled Regis around the streets trying to find his house. They stopped in front of a church and propped Regis up on the welcome sign. As they looked around trying to find something familiar, Regis throw up again. This time it was all over the welcome sign of the church.

"Well its hell for sure now," William said.

They grabbed Regis and made their way down another street. This time it was the right one. They walked up to Regis's house and found it locked. They searched Regis for keys but could not find any. At that point Regis could not even talk, so he was of no help. They stood at his door for a minute and thought about what to do.

"His car is right here," Marcus said. "Let's just sleep it off there." William was in no mood to argue. At least they could lock the doors.

So, they piled into Regis unlocked car and set him in the back. Marcus sat in the driver's seat, and William in the passenger seat. William locked the door and faded off to sleep. His first night in New Orleans sleeping in a car.

CHAPTER 11

The Colonel woke up early with the morning light just hovering over the horizon. In the middle latitudes the days are just about equal in daylight. The palm trees gently swayed back and forth outside of this window in the morning breeze. Given that he had lived there his whole life, he had gotten into a routine where he could wake up at the same time with no alarm clock. Peering out the window he could see the light starting to cross the square.

The town was just beginning to stir. People were setting up their carts for the morning influx of people wanting to buy fresh fruit before heading off to work. He laid there for a moment. Each building was painted a pastel color that the tropical sun had faded and cracked. The peeling paint gave the square an old look that added to its charm. The Colonel steeled himself for the day ahead. It had been a long time in the making, and it was finally here.

This was going to be a big day. The people had rallied to him in his call for new power, and today was the day he started to use it. Over the last couple of days, the government had been compiling a list of names, and business, that were unfriendly to the Colonel. These were the people that were about to rounded up. They would be held, without bail, for whatever period of time that was necessary to convince them of their error. About a half dozen businesses were to be closed including two small newspapers that had the audacity to print the truth. With those shuttered, and the people quieted, the Colonel could erase all the remaining opposition in one day. Then he would proclaim to the people that he had begun to clean up the island. Of course, this was only the beginning. He knew that once in power, one must convince the masses that protection is always needed. The fear can never go away. His push against the opposition was only just starting. Much time was needed in order to ensure the island was safe. The people would need to understand that more was necessary, and their leader would be there to provide it for them.

The plan was simple. His men were to leave early. They would wake the people out of their beds and have them in jail before most people had started their day. The orders were already out there, and the squads had begun their work before the Colonel open his eyes that morning. As the Colonel was dressed, he got his first reports of the action. All was going as planned.

"I want to be updated every hour on the progress," the Colonel said to an aide. "Nothing is too small to be told to me." He exited the room to begin a morning ritual of an hour-long breakfast. He ate at a 10-person table, but with no one else seated. The only other people in the room were the three attendants that waited on his every need. As countless people were being locked into jail cells without being told why, The Colonel was finishing up toast with jam, and a second cup of coffee.

Chris had woken up to guards going in and out of the holding area. Something was going on, but he could not quiet tell what it was. They had been making room in the holding area for what Chris thought would be another round up. The jail was already crowded with people who had been sitting for days, or sometimes weeks. It was just a matter of time until there was no space left. Chris did not want to think what would happen at that point. They had been holding most people by themselves, but with the additions getting ready to come in Chris thought that at some point he would get a roommate.

Throughout the morning a new arrival would be taken through the door. Usually, with a pretty surprised look on his face. Most of these people did not know what was going on and would not be told for a few days. Chris had been special in his meeting with the Colonel. No one else had the privilege of such a meeting. Most were just taken to small rooms and asked about who they knew, or places meeting were taking place. There was a bit of roughing up going on, but mostly it was just the shock of being taken away from home and family. Some would yell, others would cry, but most just keep worry at bay with a combination of strength, and patience.

Chris's guess was right. After watching the new arrivals come in for a few minutes, one in particular caught his eye. He was a small man, about five foot four, and could not have weighed over a buck ten. Chris had met him a couple of times in meetings over the last few weeks. He was not a leader of anything but was a person who knew what the Colonel was up to. Chris had known it was just a matter of time until the government caught up with men like him.

The guards were not patient today. With all of the comings and goings, people were being stashed in any place they could find. One of the guards had the small man, and was looking around for a cell to put him in. Once he saw that Chris was by himself the guard put the man in. The door slammed shut and the guard went off to process the next victim of the Colonel's roundup. The small man sat on the floor and did not even look at Chris. It did not seem that he was too surprised to be there unlike many of the others that day.

"What is your name?" Chris asked in Spanish. The man looked over and had a puzzled look on his face. Chris did not know if it was because he was a gringo sitting in a Costa Rican jail, or because of his Spanish. However, there was no response.

"My name is Chris," he tried again. "I am from the U.S." The statement did not even get a look from the small man. Chris had been held for a few days without anyone to talk to, or any word from the outside. He was a bit disappointed that the first chance he got to talk to someone was going nowhere because no one wanted to talk back. Chris decided to let it go, and just leave the guy alone.

They waited together in silence for the rest of the day. The stream of people that had started the morning was over by the afternoon. Chris guessed that there were only so many peo-ple on the island that were opposed to the Colonel that it only took a half day to bring them all in. Every once in a while, Chris would notice someone he had met. They would see him, but not respond. The small man in the cell looked at everyone the guards brought passed, but never said a word.

The evening meal had been served. A cold bowl of soup, and a bit of bread. Sometimes there would even be a little fruit in the bowl, but not this night. After the meal was served, many times the guards left the prisoners alone. None of the guards seemed to care who, or why, anyone was there. Chris did not really blame them. Most of them looked like they were about twenty years old. Only the officers were older. Chris knew that soon they would turn the lights out, and the prisoners would be left on their own for the night. He hoped it would be possible to get a little more information out of his new friend as the night went on.

Darkness fell, and the murmur of conversation could be heard all through the cell block. The cells were scorching hot during the day. Finally, when the sun started to set, and night fell, the area cooled off. Given the amount of people brought in the jail, and that the amount of space to put them did not change, now numerous people who had been by themselves for days now had someone to talk to. Chris did not. The small man just sat there looking out of the bars at a blank wall. Chris tried a couple of times to ask questions, but still got no response. So Chris just started talking. Mostly in Spanish, but since he did not think the small man was really listening, he spoke in English some of the time.

"I guess I will start telling you how I got here," Chris said as he sat back against the cold wall and started his story. At least he had someone to talk to instead of talking to himself. Sure enough Chris talked about where he had come from and how he got in that cell. He talked about his childhood, school, sports, and anything to pass the time. He had hoped that sooner or later the small man would jump in and at least give his name. Chris tried talking about himself, America, Costa Rica, baseball, but nothing worked. He even started to just talk nonsense to see if the small man would bat an eye. None of it worked.

Chris had spoken for more than an hour before he stopped. Not that he had run out of things to say, but that he got tired of talking at someone instead of talking to someone. Chris gave up, and just looked over at the small man sitting in the cell not more than six feet away from him. It figured that out of all the people they could have put in the cell, they chose one that would not talk. Chris thought for a moment that maybe he could not talk, or maybe he did not speak Spanish or English. He was alone again.

It began to get late, and the newness of having a friend in the cell was waning around the block. The sound of people talking started to slow, and the prisoners prepared for bed. Chris had gotten his mat ready and was about to pull his thin blanket over his shoulders when the small man moved toward him. He sat down remarkably close to Chris and looked at him. It was as if he was studying him. For a moment Chris was scared of what the man might do. However, he quickly realized that he was sizing him up. Almost two minutes went by in silence as the small man looked at Chris.

"My name is Davi," the small man said. "I am from the town." Chris did not know what town he meant but was not in the mood to ask many questions.

"I have seen you before," Davi said. "Where have I seen you?" It was more than a question; it was a test. Chris could only remember one time in which he saw Davi at a meeting. It was in the back of a bakery off the center square. Nothing unusual happened there. Just a meeting of disgruntled business owners complaining of the police asking for free food and money. Chris could not remember anything special about Davi at the meeting. He was not even sure that he spoke.

"I know we attended a meeting together," Chris replied slowly. "I can't remember where it was, but I do remember seeing you there." There was another moment of silence.

"What were you doing there?" Davi asked.

"I was just trying to see how I could help." Davi was trying to see if there was anything to fear in Chris. By nature, one had to be skeptical of others. Given the state of the island, trust was a tough thing to come by. Davi wondered if Chris were planted in the jail because no one would think anything of him or was he just a hopeful American down in the banana republic's trying to make a difference.

Davi and Chris started to speak. Chris was eager to talk, and Davi was a bit more hesitant. Chris went through how he ended up in jail, and Davi explained why there were so many more people showing up. Slowly trust began to build.

"It's a roundup," he told Chris. "Anyone the Colonel thinks is against him will be here. Some only for a little while, but others will stay for a much longer time."

"Which one are you?" asked Chris.

"I plan to be here for a while," Davi said with a smile. Chris thought for a moment.

"Which one am I?" he asked.

"I don't know, but I will hope for you."

The two started talking about their lives and homes. Davi had a family in town that was very worried about what would happen to him. He had told them that he may have to go away for a while. A few days before his arrest he sent his family to the mainland to stay with relative. From there he just waited until the police came.

"I think I might have a way out," Chris blurted out after the family stories were done. Davi looked surprised and waited for Chris to tell his story.

"I sent a letter to a friend," Chris started. "I told them that I might be in some trouble down here. Things were getting a little out of hand before they brought me here. So I mailed a letter to a guy who I thought could help me out."

"And what became of that letter?" Davi asked.

"I don't know. I sent it the day before they picked me up. I don't know if it got there or not," Chris seemed a little down about the prospects of the letter doing much of anything.

"It could amount to nothing," Chris finally said. Davi looked at Chris and saw that he was not looking forward to his near future.

"I have been sizing you up all day," Davi started. "I didn't know if they would put me in a cell with someone who would just try and get information out of me in order to help themselves. However, you do not seem to have anything that they could offer, and I am not afraid." Chris gave him a look of thanks.

"So what options do we have?" Chris asked.

"Not many," Davi said with a slight laugh. "I have no friends to mail a letter. They are all in here or gone."

"If it does get to him, all he has to do is find the Leopard," Chris said. "He will know how to get us out of here."

"Ah, the Leopard," Davis said as he leaned back against the wall. Chris looked over at him and thought he saw a faint smile start to cross his face.

CHAPTER 12

It took them a couple of days in order to sort things out. William was impatient to get moving, but it was not that easy. Marcus and Regis were in no hurry to head south. Regis had a couple of last-minute things to put together before they left. He would not tell William what they were, and William did not really want to push the subject. Marcus tried to get William to go out and see some of the sights of New Orleans. He did not manage to get him to walk around St. Louis cemetery and look at the graves.

Given that the United State was relatively young for a country, the graves of New Orleans gave an antique flavor to the city that many other cities could not replicate. They took a daytime walk through the French Quarter to check out the funky shops. The Quarter at night was lively with throngs of people drinking in their merriment, with music and revelry hanging in the air.

However, the morning was different. Quiet streets devoid of people, the hot humid air broken by a soft coolness that calmed the streets seemed to sedate the people. William tried to be patient and enjoy his new surroundings. Despite all around him he could not get the thought out of his head that Chris was in real need of help. Marcus promised him that they would leave the next day.

Marcus had been looking for flights to Costa Rica, and found one leaving the next morning. William hated to admit it but taking a couple of days to figure out a plan was not such a waste of time. They still did not know what they were going to run into when they finally reached Costa Rica.

They would pack lite because they did not know where they were going to go, or for how long. Each of them had a backpack that could be taken on the place as a carryon.

"I am not going to wait around for checked bags, just to haul them around Central America," Marcus said. "The rule is pack light." Everyone agreed and got everything they needed into the bags. William had gotten used to traveling with little.

That night the three guys sat around Regis kitchen table to discuss the plan.

"So, over the next couple of days we are going to have to fly, drive, and boat to get to Chris," Marcus told them.

"Planes, trains, and Automobiles," said Regis.

"No trains Regis," William told him. Regis looked puzzled for a moment, and then realized his mistake. Marcus was going to get them into San Jose, the Capital of Costa Rica. They would stay there for a night before heading to the coast. He had found a driver named Peter who took people to the Coast. Peter would pick them up early in the morning after they arrived. Once on the west coast they would make their way over to the island and find Chris. Along the way they hoped to figure out what the Leopard was, and what to do with it. However, none of them knew the first thing about finding the Leopard.

"I don't understand how we are going to find Chris, or the Leopard?" Regis asked.

"We will just have to feel it out once we get there," Marcus replied. "Chris didn't give us much to go on."

"We need to figure out what the problem with Chris is in the first place," William told the other. They all agreed that finding Chris would be first, and then they would work from there.

The morning was crisp given the usual heat of New Orleans that time of year. The guys got a taxi and headed toward the airport. William was once again in the position of having to fly. Even though he had just stepped off a plane a few days prior, the experience did not get any easier. The taxi did not take long to make it to the departure entry of the airport. Each of the guys carried only one small bag to by-pass the hassle of having to claim baggage in a foreign country.

Marcus had already printed out their tickets, so they passed through security, and made their way to the plane. William looked anxiously at the plane before they boarded.

"You O.K.?" Asked Regis.

"Just don't like flying," William replied.

"Want a drink to ease your nerves?"

"No" Replied William remembering how he felt on the last flight given Marcus solution to ease his nerves. He would just have to get through this one. The flight had been delayed for some time, so William walked around the airport, and found a bookstore. Looking around the store he spotted a book on Costa Rica and decided to get it for the plane ride. Now all he could do was wait.

Finally, after a few hours of waiting for the plane to arrive, they saw it pull up to the loading area. The passengers got off the plane, and the airline announced that they would be boarding shortly.

They boarded the plane and took their seats. The weather was good leaving the State and the flight was easy. William was able to relax a bit and turn his attention to a book about Costa

Rica he had bought in the airport. It went through the history of the country and had a section about each region. William looked at the west coast given that is where they would be heading. He had never been to Central America before, and was excited to see something new. The pages of pictures showed coffee growing on hillsides and spoke about the surfing on the coast. William doubted there would be time for surfing, but the pictures of the Pacific Coast looked beautiful.

The flight was to last about four hours. They would be shooting straight down over the Gulf of Mexico into Central America. Day was turning to night as the boys made their way down to the single latitudes. William felt a bit better this time. Maybe it was because he had just flown, but he did not need to be knocked out with drugs. William knew that most of the flight was over, and they would be in San Jose shortly. Once they neared the airport in San Jose the captain came over the speaker.

"The airport in San Jose has zero visibility," he said. "We have been instructed to hold until further notice." There was a groan from the passengers as all knew they would be delayed in getting to their hotels. William sat back in his seat and tried not to let it bother him. A little delay is no big deal he thought to himself.

They circled for about 20 minutes until the Captain again started to speak.

"We have been told to proceed to the Liberia International Airport and await further instructions." William got his book out and saw that there was a little airport in the Northwest corner of Costa Rica named Liberia.

"Welcome to Central America," Marcus said out loud. The plane made a sharp turn toward the west and headed into the dying sun. Within minutes they were making their descent into Liberia International Airport. Night had fallen and the stars had come out. The plane pulled up to a building that must have been the airport. There were not any other planes around except for a few turbo props outside of a hanger.

"I guess this is it," William said, relieved that they were finally on the ground. At least now they could just get out and find their way to the coast.

"We can just figure it out from here," Marcus said thinking they were about to get off the plane. Just then the Captain came back on.

"Everyone just sit tight," he said. "We have been told to sit here until visibility is better in San Jose. We will then return to that airport." William was not happy to be sitting on a plane waiting to fly again.

"Since we have the time, the Flight Attendants will be coming around with drinks to make your unexpected stop-over a bit better." There was a cheer from the back of the plane where a group of 50-year-old were sitting. It looked to William like some sort of class reunion given the group took up four rows of seats and all had on matching Hawaiian print shirts.

The Flight Attendant did come around serving drinks to the passengers. William was tempted to get one but thought better of it. Time went by and the passengers got restless. Many asked if they could just get out and go into the airport. After over an hour on the ground the Captain addressed the issue.

"I have contacted airport officials and requested permission to disembark," he started. "However, we have been told that all of the customs officials in Liberia have gone home for the evening, and there would be no one to process you into the Country." Therefore, they sat on the plane. After about another thirty minutes the Margaritaville party in the back was in full swing. Marcus was trying to fit in a nap, and William was about to go crazy. They had been on the plane for over six hours, and it was stretching William's ability to fly.

Regis just sat there looking around as if nothing was bothering him. Softly, he started to sing a song. It was almost under his breath, but William tried to make out the words.

"Big Old jet airliner…" he sang. He sat in his seat bobbing up and down to the words. Marcus looked over at him with a puzzled look on his face. Regis just kept singing, but this time louder and louder. The lyrics of the Boston song started to fill the cabin. People turned to look at him as he kept singing.

"Don't carry me too far away," he sang. Then others started to join in. Soon the party in the back had caught on, and most of the passengers were singing.

"Big old jet airliner, don't take me too far away…" William was temporarily broken out of his funk and joined along. Unbeknown to them the Captain had turned the intercom on and fed it to the tower in San Jose. After listening to it for a little the tower control came back and said that they could leave given the passengers sarcastic take on the situation. Even though unintended Regis' little tune worked, and they were about to get underway.

"O.K. everyone," the Captain stated. "San Jose control has told us to make our way back. Visibility has improved and they think we can make it." With that William heard the engines start up.

"What the hell does he mean they THINK we can make it?" William asked Marcus. Marcus did not answer. It was one of the few times Marcus genuinely looked frightened. The plane made its way down the runway and off into the dark sky. William had read that San Jose sat in the valley in the middle of 9000-foot-tall mountains surrounding it like a bowl.

The plane rose for only a few minutes before it started back down. As they descended through the clouds William looked out the window to see lights straight out past the wing. That meant that they were in the middle of mountains. In an instant a cloud would engulf the plane, and he could see nothing. Then, out of nowhere, the lights would appear. The plane would bounce once it hit the cloud.

There were long moments where William could see nothing out the window. Regis sat in his seat and closed his eyes. Marcus would look out the window, and then when the cloud hit would look straight down at the floor. Even though seated in the back, the party had not stopped, and cheers could be heard every time the cloud lifted, and jeers when it returned. William was quite certain at that point he was going to die in a plane crash. He was almost calm he was so sure.

Everyone could tell that they were getting close to the ground. The lights became numerous and started to blanket the side of the mountains and the ground. That is when they could see the ground. The Captain pulled the flaps up and raised the nose. William looked out the window and suddenly a cloud blanketed the sky. It was over and he knew it. Then the cloud lifted, and as soon as it did the wheels hit the ground with a thud. It was a hard landing, and everyone was thrown a bit forward. The engines were reversed, and the plane started to slow. Cheers went up from the passengers including William.

The plane made its way to the terminal and pulled up to the gate. As each of the passengers got off of the plane, they said thank you to the crew. No one was happier than William. The boys were finally in Costa Rica.

CHAPTER 13

Once they were on the ground in San Jose, William was relieved. They disembarked the plane and made it through the long line at customs. Even though it was almost midnight, there was a long line waiting to make it through. The airport spit them out on the street where, even though late at night, there were taxis lined up. The word was that you should only take a certain colored taxi. Those were the ones that had been checked out by the government. William wondered how anyone was supposed to know this. Looking at the brightly colored cars in front of him, he wondered what shade of color was safe. Some looked orange, off orange, and light red. Marcus knew which one to take and made his way to an orange taxi. He told him the name of the hotel, and the three were on their way.

There was not much to see in the darkness. Out the window William could see buildings and what looked like a tooth paste factory. The place did not look bad, maybe not the same as downtown Chicago, but nothing that he would have called the derogatory name of third world. Some places didn't' look any different than places he saw back in the States. William was just happy to be out of the airplane. Even though they were stuck in a small car, he was on the ground, and making his way to a bed.

It did not take them long to get to their hotel. A non-descript building on the outside with comfortable rooms on the inside. It was better than some of the places he stayed in Europe. William was tired from the long journey and wanted to get to bed. They sat their stuff down and picked beds. Marcus was looking at something on the internet.

"What is that?" Regis asked.

"I am setting up a guy to take us to the coast tomorrow," Marcus said. "We need to get moving."

"Nothing early," William said as he laid down on the bed.

"Right, nothing early." Soon it was lights out, and time for sleep.

The much-needed rest did them all good. Marcus was true to this word and did not set up the ride until almost lunch time. William woke up and headed out to explore the hotel. There was a small courtyard in the middle with tropical looking trees that he had never seen. There were chairs scattered around so he grabbed one and sat down. It was good to just sit down and look around. With no one else in the courtyard, William was alone with his thoughts. There had not been much time to think since they had left Italy. Since there was no plan William tried to think of what to do next. They needed to make it over to the island, but he could not think of what to do after that.

Before he had left Maria had told him no phone calls. William had agreed. Mostly because they both knew that it would cost a small fortune to make even a two-minute call halfway around the world. So William got out his phone and sent her an e-mail. He had promised to check it every now and then. Maria had told him she just wanted to know everyone was alright. Thankfully, she never wanted any details of what was going on. Once done he sat back to wait until departure time and think about how to find Chris.

About a half an hour of sitting and thinking, without any results, was enough. William was still stuck on what to do. He hoped that maybe it would just find them. He headed back to the room and grabbed his stuff.

Marcus and Regis were up and almost ready to head out. He did not know if they had even been out of the room, but both looked rested and refreshed.

"Car will be here in twenty minutes," Marcus said. "We are going to grab something to eat, and head down."

"I'll be down in a minute," William said being the only one who never ate anything for breakfast. The guys went out, and William took a very fast shower in the exceedingly small bathroom. He got dressed and headed down to the lobby. There was Marcus talking to a man in his forties dressed in khaki pants and a tan polo shirt.

"This is Peter," Marcus said. "He will be our ride to the coast."

"Hello!" Peter said in English extending his hand. "Are you ready to get going?" They shook hands and started out the door. The ride was a full-size van modified to take about eight people. This was a private hire by Marcus, so it was only going to be the four of them riding. Marcus sat up front with Peter, with Regis in the back, and William in the middle row.

They took off through San Jose zipping in and out of traffic as they headed west. It was mid-morning, and the traffic going out of the city was not that bad. William looked at the passing scenery that varied from green fields to moderate housing developments. They rode northwest up what Americans would call the Pan-American Highway. All along the way Peter would describe the area around them. As they started to get outside the city the view changed. Off in the distance Peter pointed out the volcano Poas reaching up towards the clouds. The world outside turned greener, and hills and mountains surrounded the valley. Given the many twists and turns the road had to take, the progress was slow. However, that gave William time to look around and take in the different views.

As they rode, they passed small towns with small homes, and small businesses. There were people walking around and taking care of the day-to-day things that all must do. Nothing seemed all together shabby about any of the places they went through. Most of all it seemed peaceful. Not at all like a country that would kidnap and hold his friend.

The road slowed as they moved toward the coast. There was no way to go directly west in Costa Rica. The mountains created a barrier against a straight shot. The van started to climb as William could see coffee and banana fields spread out before him. Beans clung to the mountainside as they made their way through the switchbacks up the mountain. Every now and then there would be blind curves, and traffic on both sides. Peter was an expert at getting the van to fit around the tight corners where any miscalculation could leave you going over the Cliffside. The clouds started to get closer as they made their way through the mountains, and over to the coast. Fields gave way to rain forests on the other side. Small town dotted the road, with a gas station, or random eating establishment showing up every few miles.

After a couple of hours on the road, the guys were ready for a break. They asked Peter when they could get out and stretch their legs and were told that he already had an idea of a place to stop. It was only a few more minutes, and they would get out. It was a river crossing, and he wanted to show them something they had probably never seen. That was good enough for William.

True to his word after about fifteen more minutes the van slowed and pulled over to the side. There was a few houses and shops around, but not much to call a town. The houses lined the road about fifty yards away from the river. William looked around and saw people carrying various items up and down the road. Other than the houses there was nothing but trees and forest.

"Where are we?" Asked Regis as he tumbled out of the van.

"This is the river Tarcoles" Peter said proudly as he made a wide gesture with his arms. It was as if he was presenting a new car on a TV show. "Just wait there is a surprise at the bridge." So, they followed Peter the fifty yards to the bridge over the Rio Tarcloes. Peter walked out onto the bridge and looked over. William followed him and peered over down to the water. To his surprise two dozen very large alligators lay at the bottom.

"Holy crap!" Said Regis as he got his first look. "Look at the size of those. Can we go down there?" Marcus and William looked at Regis like he was a crazy man.

"People don't go down there," said Peter, trying not to look like a man explaining something obvious. He explained that it was a highly polluted river, and that normally no one would actually go into it.

"But there is something we can do that is fun."

The guys followed Peter off the bridge as he walked to the collection of houses and shops by the van. William guessed that the bridge was a stopping off point to many travelers in the area, and the shops had popped up to gather that business. It was not necessarily a lively place, but at least there was something interesting to do. Peter walked over to a three-sided shack with a fenced off area to the side. A small woman was sitting at a table mending a piece of clothing. Peter and the women exchanged some words in rapid fire Spanish.

"I need a 50 Colons," Peter said to William.

"Why do you need money?"

"I need it to buy the chicken," he replied.

"What the hell do we need with a chicken?" William asked him as he handed over the money.

"You will see my friend," was his reply. He took the money from William and handed it to the woman. Without a word she motioned him over to the yard where the chickens were pecking at the ground. Peter opened the gate and went in. He stood for a moment without making a move, until one of the chickens came near him. He quickly grabbed it by the neck and left the pen.

"Follow me," he told the guys. Not knowing what was going on each of them got into a line behind him as he made his way back to the bridge. At the bridge he gathered all of the guys around him. Some of the people on the bridge were curious what the man with the chicken was doing and came over for a look.

"Now watch." He then tossed the chicken over the side of the bridge. Down it crashed towards the water below. After a few seconds it landed right in the middle of the alligators. Soon enough there was nothing left of the chicken as a couple of the alligators tore it to pieces. William was not faint of heart, nor were either of the other two, but this was not their thing. Peter looked at them studying their reactions. It was not what he expected. The three of them stood in silence looking at each other not knowing what to do, or what to say. A couple of obvious Americans were standing by and cried out as the chicken was eaten.

"Well, that is a first for me," Regis said as he turned and walked back toward the van.

"I thought you guys would want to see something different," Peter said. "I bet you don't find that back in America." It did not seem to bother him that he just through a chicken over a bridge to its death.

"I guess you could say that," William said as he got back in the van. The guys did not know whether to laugh or be horrified. It was certainly something that they would not forget.

"I guess that is about the same as what happens every day at a chicken restaurant," Regis said.

"Where do you eat?" Marcus asked, raising is eyebrows at Regis.

Shortly after the chicken sacrifice the boys got back on the road. Peter said it would not be much longer until they reached the hotel. Marcus had made arraignments at a place that would be the taking off point to get to the island. It was a complex of hotels and houses along the Pacific coast. Marcus saw no reason that they should not stay somewhere nice while trying to rescue their friend.

With rain forests on one side and the Pacific Ocean on the other, William was fascinated by the scenery. They were riding down a two-lane road that hugged the coast. There were not many cars on the road giving the ride a lonely feeling. The green canvass of trees covered the mountains to his left, as the waters of the Pacific died on the beaches to his right. The sun was starting it is decent into the waters to the west. It was just about as peaceful of a place William had ever seen. Peter was a terrific guide through the country. He knew the tress, and plants along the road. He told short histories of the small towns they drove through and was quiet when the scenery was doing the talking.

The entrance to the hotel complex was a gate with a guardhouse. Palm trees lined the road as the van pulled up to the lonely guard at the gate. Peter showed him the pass, and they were on their way in matter of minutes. Even with the setting sun's dime light, William could see the beautiful surroundings as they headed into the complex. It was set on 2000 acres of land that had been a part of a national rainforest of Costa Rica. By agreement, the hotel was to maintain the surroundings as they were so that wildlife could flourish. It was a slow drive up the road toward the main house. A canopy of trees and vegetation covered them as they made their way. It gave the drive a dark enclosed feeling. After a few minutes, the darkness gave way to a bit lighter as the canopy opened up to a well-maintained land-scape. A modest building resembling a house stood before them. Peter pulled up to the open-air counter.

"Here you are," he said as he turned off the van. Everyone got out with Peter and Marcus settling up the payment. William was surprised at how early the sun went down in Costa Rica.

"It's pretty much like that the whole year," Peter said when he asked him about it. "We are so close to the Equator that the daylight stays pretty much the same the whole year. Around 6:00 pm the sun sets, and around 6:00 am it comes up again." He gave a shrug of his shoulders as if to say that is just how it is.

Peter drove away after giving everyone in the party one of his cards in case there was a return visit. Marcus headed toward the desk to check them in. William and Regis decided to walk around to see what was there. The place was huge so they could not see it all, but there was a nice pool with an outdoor bar, and a restaurant a few yards away.

"What the hell is that?" Regis exclaimed as he jumped almost three feet in the air.

"What is what?" William replied.

"That!" William looked ahead and, in the dim, light made out something on the ground. He walked closer to find that a large lizard was sitting in the middle of the walkway. The thing had to be two feet long. Longer than any lizard William had come in contact with.

"Just stay away from it, and it won't bother you," William said. "Let us get back and find Marcus. Without a word Regis started back without taking his eyes off the lizard. They made their way back to the desk where Regis had to ask the guy behind the counter about the lizard.

"They will not bother you. Just stand clear of them, and don't make any sudden movements toward them." It was not as reassuring as Regis would have hoped.

It was a bit of a walk to the room. Down a path, and past a huge tree with a sign that stated it was 400 years old. As darkness fell William could still make out the bright vibrant flowers hanging from the nearby trees. Colors were everywhere including an ominous flash of lightening off in the distance. Finally, they got to the room. The room was not much other than a basic hotel room in groups of four in a building. They went in and set their stuff down. William laid down on the bed and thought about what was going to take place the next day.

The reason Marcus picked the hotel was that it was only about three miles from the ferry that would take them to the island. They would catch a ride to the terminal and take the one-hour ride to the island to find Chris. They had no idea on how to find him but decided that William would be the one to talk. They would pretend to be from the US consulate office and were checking in on citizens in the area. They would poke around asking about a few people, only one would be real. Hopefully, no one would be able to tell what they were up to, and they would find Chris. William was not sure it was a good idea, but it was the only idea they had that made sense.

"What do we do about me not speaking Spanish?" William asked.

"That is where your translator comes in," Marcus said pointing at Regis

"You don't think it might look a little strange that an Assistant American Consult must use a translator?"

"Let's hope they don't think that much into it," Marcus said.

Thunder boomed closer and closer as William lay on the bed looking at the ceiling. He mostly hoped that this was a misunderstanding, and they would find Chris at some seaside bar with a big smile on his face. However, there was a nagging feeling that something was not right, and they were getting into something bigger. Marcus and Regis looked out the window as rain started to fall. There was not much conversation, nor the need for much. Things had been talked over, and now it was just time to act. The rain poured and landed loudly on the roof of the building. It was nothing like any of them had ever heard. They opened the door and looked out at the storm. The rain was coming in heavy now. The guys worried that it was not normal and that they may have to make a run for it. Thinking better of it they told each other that is was just a part of staying right next to a rainforest, and that they better get used to it. It was just one of the many things a person must get used to when traveling in a new country. They were to get up early the next morning to catch the first ferry over to the island. Each of them picked a place to sleep, and with the storm still raging outside, tried to get some sleep.

CHAPTER 14

The island tour was one of the things the Colonel loved to do. He got to put on his nicest uniform, get in his best car, and drive around telling people how good of a job he was doing. Given that one could get around the whole island in a long day, it was his chance to get out and be back in the safety of his capital the very same day. Everyone knew the routine. At 7:00 am the Colonel would be up and ready to go. The uniform was to be laid out, and the car was to be ready. Everyone in the building would be in a rush except for the Colonel. There was always time for a breakfast. However, once he was ready to go, everyone else was expected to be ready to move.

As he exited the building guards with guns gleaming would snap to attention, and the car door would open. After a crisp salute, the Colonel would be off. It was much like a military inspection, of course, without the military. There would be several cars. All of them black, and mostly shinny. The lead car would be full of personal guards for the Colonel. That was followed by a varying sort of military vehicle. There were not many on the island for obvious reasons, so the Colonel had to improvise. There would be the usual cars full of hangers-on making the procession a reasonably large one. Police would hold all other traffic at a standstill while the Colonel made it out of town.

The Colonel had stuffed himself into his bedazzled uniform and was comfortably seated in the back of his car. It was already hot, with morning temperatures already above 80. The guards did their best jammed into the vehicles around him.

Much of what they would do was set up during the previous few days by those loyal to the Colonel. There would be meetings with the people of the small towns that dotted the outer edges of the island. The Colonel would give a short pre-prepared speech, and then give handshakes to a very small amount of selected citizens. After that everyone would be packed back into the cars and sped off to the next destination. The speeches to crowds of people who were there only because after the government would distribute free food to all those who stayed. A few minutes of standing, and listening, was not a bad trade for a free meal to most of the people. It was fake planned show, with the people as the props. All of which were set up and waiting for the Colonel to arrive.

It did not take long for the Colonel to get out of the city. In a few minutes they would be at their first stop. They pulled into the seaside village with a few buildings in the center and two docks for the boats to unload their daily catch. The Colonel's people had arranged for a dozen or so "citizens" to be there to welcome him. That they did. As he stepped out of the car a cheer went up from the small crowd. Looking at the meager turnout the Colonel was unhappy. Whoever was the unfortunate person who organized the crowd would be looking for a new job when the day was done.

The people walked the Colonel out to one of the docks where it just so happened that a boat was unloading its catch of the morning. In true to form Colonel mode, he went out to the boat and spent a minute helping to unload the fish. The fishermen in the boat were somewhat surprised at such help but knew better than to ask questions. A few pictures were taken, and a short speech made. At least since the cars pulled up people got curious as to what was going on. Therefore, the crowd was a bit larger as the Colonel sped away. Even with the small crowd he deemed it a success.

The day went on pretty much the same as the first. There was the Colonel helping kids in a school, helping old ladies buy food, and pretending to listen when people had a problem. They would all be forgotten in a matter of hours. The point was to be seen as a man of the people without having to actually do anything for the people. The weather was hot, but clear. With the twenty pounds of uniform the Colonel was carrying around, the heat was taking its toll.

"Only one more stop," the Colonel told his driver. "I have enough for only one more." This happened from time to time. Some days he would go to a dozen towns. Other days only four or five. If anyone was missed, they were told to just go home. This day would be no different.

The last stop would be a small village on the other side of the island. There were not many people living there, so the Colonel knew it could be quick. He did not really like going out this far in the sticks, but his advisors told him it would be best to make a show. So with the afternoon in full swing the car pulled up next to a collection of fruit stands, and makeshift shops. People were milling about, but one could not tell if they were there to see the Colonel, or just because milling around is what they did all day. However, in the mind of the Colonel they were all there to see him. Given the large lunch he had before entering the town, it was lucky the Colonel could even get out of the car. He popped out like a cork from a well shaken bottle of Champaign to the awaiting crowd. There was not much to do in this town. There were no fish, no school, not really anything. So with a rhetorical flourish that showed this was his last stop of the day, the Colonel launched one last time into his speech. He did not even get more than ten feet away from the car this time. He could tell there were many faces looking at them but was concentrating too much on talking to care who they actually were. With a wave of his hat he was back in his car and heading out. There was applause from the crowd, and free food to be handed out, but that was for someone else to worry about. It was time for the Colonel to get back to his light clothes, good food, and soft bed.

The vehicles were packed tight again and began to move off back toward town. The Colonel had already opened a bottle of chilled wine for the ride home. His car was the only one with working air conditioning, making his ride as comfortable as possible. There was no such luck for all of those with him. They rode home baking in the heat, with no food or wine, to make the ride home a bit more enjoyable.

Out of sight at the last stop stood a man watching the last car pull out of town. He was no more than thirty yards from the Colonel when his car passed. He was old, a nice white beard hung from his face. A closer look would have told you that he was a gringo. No one seemed to be paying much attention to him. He looked like a great many baby boomers trying to live out a fantasy life in the tropics. Other than that, nothing stood out in his appearance. That is exactly how he wanted it. He had been around for a while now and did not need any unwanted attention.

CHAPTER 15

The Morning was bright, and sunny, as the boys waited at the dock for the ferry to arrive. They had gotten up early in order to have a little breakfast, and head out. There was not much of a town other than the dock. A few intrepid businessmen decided to try their lot at serving travelers waiting for the ferry. Nothing more than shacks had been set up to do the work. William had walked over to one of these shops and looked inside. Satisfied that he could find something to eat, he went inside.

"Hello," William said to the man behind the counter. He did not reply. William looked around, and found a banana, and a piece of fruit he could not identify. He bought the fruit, and a cup of what was put up as coffee and headed out. Marcus and Regis had wandered out by the dock with their own food.

"Not a bad morning," Marcus said as William came up to them.

"I have seen worse," William replied, and so he had. The sun was rising above the trees behind them, and the Pacific stretched out in front of them. Their next stop was the island.

William was not sure what they thought they would do when they got to the island. Neither Marcus, nor Regis, had said anything about a master plan. However, William was happy that they were finally going to be on the island. It seemed like they were making some progress. The three of them waited for a while as the boat was readied for the trip. William would have liked to know what was going to happen next, but he knew that the only way to find out was to move forward.

The ferry docked in the mid-morning. It was not as big of a boat as William would have liked. He did not have a fear of the water, but he knew that they would have to be on this thing for a while. There were a dozen or so people waiting to get on. The guys were the only non-natives to be taking a ride that day, although no one seemed to care. For a few dollars they had their seats and were about to be on their way. There was not much room to get up and move around so the guys just found seats together and figured they would sit it out.

The engines fired up, and the ferry made its way from the dock. It headed out to sea toward an un-seen island over the horizon. It was a bit bumpy at first, but after a few miles the ride smoothed out. It was a beautiful day to be out on the water. While not making fast progress, the ferry was holding up and looked like it had a good chance to make its destination.

"Who are we going to ask about Chris when we get there?" Regis inquired. "I mean it's not like we know anyone here."

"I would just go to the local police station, and if they don't know anything, then the hospital," said William. Other than that, he figured they would just have to walk around and see if anyone knew anything.

"What do you think his problem is?" Regis asked.

"I don't know," Marcus replied. "The letter didn't really say much about what was going wrong. Just that there was something going wrong." William thought about the Warren Zevon song about Lawyers, guns, and money. They certainly would need some of that in the next couple of days.

"Let's just see what happens when we get there," William said.

The ride was better than William had expected. Time passed slowly as he watched the open water on their way to the island. After an hour, the island came into view slowly. A small dot in the middle of the water started to get larger and larger. Finally, the ferry pulled up to a dock in what had to have been the main town on the island. The guys got off the boat and made their way into the town. William was struck by the combination of beauty and hustle of the place. There was the Pacific Ocean stretching out before them with different types of boats tied up ready for launch. Store fronts were open selling fresh fish, and fruits to passersby. There was a sense of purpose and movement in the town, but not a hurried one. The streets were not clean, at least as clean as he had seen on the mainland. There were many more boarded up storefronts, and derelict buildings on the street for a country that prided itself on being a stable economy. The stream of tourists heading into Costa Rica had obviously not made it this far.

"OK Regis this is where your talents come into play," William said.

"You didn't bring me along for nothing."

They made their way into the crowd. It seemed as if most of the people on the island decided to congregate at the very same place. There was money to be made off the people exiting the boat. A ferry came over to the island twice a day, and each time deposited potential customers at the dock. Not very many tourists came out this far, but some did. Those who did make it were immediately accosted by numerous venders for things such as sightseeing trips to fresh fish. This was no different for three, rather pathetic looking, Americans just off the boat.

"They think we have money," Regis said as three men came up to him speaking rapid fire Spanish. He replied that he was not interested, but it did no good.

"Remember, in comparison to them we do have money," William replied.

"Well, get them over to Marcus, he is the one with the money."

"I don't think they will understand, but I will try." Marcus and William were having an even worse time. Neither of them spoke Spanish so they could not understand a word that was being said.

"Regis, can you find a place we can sit down and collect our thoughts," Marcus said. "We can't figure out what to do if we just stand here being yelled at by these people."

"Why do I have to figure it out?"

"Because you speak Spanish!" Frustrated at his newfound responsibility Regis moved along trying to find a bar to sit down. A little way down the street there was a place with an open front that they could just walk into. It was called the Sand Box in relation to its proximity to a small beach across the street. The guys ducked in leaving a trail of vendors behind them.

"What the hell do we do now?" Regis asked as they sat down.

"We need to find a government building," William said. "At least then we can figure out if there are any records of Chris. Then we will go look at the local hospital to see if he has been admitted. After that police stations, and anyone else that looks like they may know something."

"What do we do just walk in and say we came down here to find a friend that sent us a letter saying he was in trouble?" Marcus asked.

"I haven't thought of that yet."

"Turn on your lawyer brain."

"I did and you already owe me $500."

The guys ordered beers and tried to plan their next move. William wanted to take the obvious route. They should just find the nearest government office and inquire about how to find a friend on the island. Costa Rica was a welcoming country and would probably try and help if they could. After that they would just have to look around until they found something.

"Regis, I need you to talk to the bartender, or owner, about where the nearest government office is that could help us."

"What do I say?"

"Just ask them where a city administrative building is because we are trying to find a friend. We do not need them to know everything. We just need to know how to get in touch with someone in charge."

Regis took a drink of his beer and headed toward the bar. William and Marcus could not hear what they were saying, but it did not look as easy as they thought it would be. After a few minutes Regis came back to the table.

"What did he say?" Asked William

"He said that he didn't know why we would go asking him about something like that."

"What does that mean?"

"I don't know but he kept asking me why we would want to go ask him something like that. When I told them we were worried about a friend, he told me that a lot of people were worried about friends around here, but you don't go asking about them." The three of them sat in silence wondering what the hell he meant by that.

"Who did he say we should talk to?"

"He really didn't say. He just kept saying we shouldn't be asking about it."

"Did he ever tell you where a government building would be?"

"Finally, at the end he said it was only a few blocks away."

"Well, let's start there," William said.

The three drank the last of the beers and headed out. They made a quick move from the front of the building to avoid attracting attention from the vendors and made their way into the town. Even though they were on the Pacific side of the country, the town had a Caribbean vibe to it. The streets were mainly sand and packed rock, and the store fronts were open to the street. People were walking and biking around. There were a few old golf carts moving around, but very few cars. There would not have been much room from them anyway. As they moved away from the docks the crowd thinned out to a smattering of people moving about town. The town looked about the same as many of the mainland towns, with maybe a bit more run-down, but island friendly feeling. The guys moved toward where the bartender said a government building would be but could not seem to find one. Finally, they saw what had to be some sort of government agency in a whitewashed building a block down the street. It did not look busy, so they walked inside.

Once inside the building they found a single room staffed by a guy in the corner watching a fuzzy television set. He did not seem too interested in their arrival. Without looking up from the T.V. he asked what they wanted. Regis dove in with questions about how to find a friend. William and Marcus stood there looking around waiting for Regis to translate. The guy at the desk did not have much information and did not look like he was going to try extremely hard to get any. After about a minute Regis stopped and walked back toward his friends.

"He said that we should go to the police station and ask about a missing person."

"That sounds reasonable."

"There was just something about him telling us to go there. Almost like we could go, but it probably wouldn't turn out too good."

"How do get all of that out of your conversation?" Asked William.

"It wasn't what he said, but the way he said it," replied Regis "I don't know, but I do know how to get there. The three of them walked out into the street and started to make their way to the police station. It was only a few blocks away given that the city was not noticeably big to begin with. The station was much bigger than any of the other buildings in the city. Next to it looked to be some sort of central government building. The two were by far the nicest buildings in the city.

They stopped outside of the entrance and wondered what to do next.

"Regis, you will have to go in. You are the only one who speaks Spanish so go and figure out if they can tell us anything," William said.

"I am not going in there by myself."

"It's a police station, what are they going to do to you."

"I have seen enough movies to know that this is how you get framed for drugs, or asked for a bribe, and then sit in jail for 10 years. I am not going in there by myself."

"Fine, we will all go in there, but we will look stupid standing there together," Marcus said as he made his way toward the entrance. As they entered the building, they came upon a waiting room of sorts. It looked like a small waiting room one would find at a hospital and smelled about the same. Regis walked up to the counter and started to speak to the officer behind the desk. There were officers of various levels milling around the place. William and Marcus stood a few feet behind Regis trying not to look like they did not know what was going on. Regis stood there and poured out his story again to the office. However, this time the officer was very interested in what he had to say. During the conversation, he waved another officer over to hear what Regis was saying. Marcus and William thought they may have hit on something given the interest shown by the officers.

Soon the conversation was over. There were now three officers talking with Regis and showing real concern for what he was saying. Regis looked back at the boys and gave a nod as if to say things were going well. He stayed at the desk waiting for an officer to tell him what to do next. Within a few minutes another officer came into the room followed by the others. He looked much more serious and marched right up to Regis. William knew that this probably was not good. With luck he thought that they could just say sorry to bother you and be on their way. From the looks of how things were now going, that was not going to be the case.

Regis was not in his element, and William and Marcus were in no place to help him. William could see that he was being pelted with questions from the man in charge. Regis was now visibly sweating, and nervous. From time to time he would point in William's direction, and each of the officers would look over for a minute, and then start talking again. This went on for about ten minutes before the ranking officer marched out of the room yelling at a couple of other officers. Regis slowly moved toward William and Marcus relieved to be out of that conversation.

"What in the hell did you say to them?" Marcus asked.

"I just told them what I have been telling everyone else. We are looking for someone, and we wondered if they could help. At first, they seemed interested in who we were, and who we were looking for. I described Chris, and it all went to hell."

"Why were they pointing at me?"

"Well, that is when I got scared. I do not know what all they said because I was nervous, and they were talking so fast. It made them mad when I asked about Chris."

"Why would that make them mad?" Asked William

"Because he is here." Marcus and William looked at each other. William was relieved that they had found Chris. Even if there was some trouble at least they knew where he was and could now figure out how to get him out.

"What do you mean he is here?" Marcus asked.

"When the other officer came in the room, he asked me why I was asking about someone they were holding here," Regis replied. "He was not happy about us coming in and asking about him."

"What did that have to do with you pointing over here?"

"I needed some reason to be here. I did not think they wanted to hear about a few friends dropping by to check on someone who was in jail. I got scared and told a lie."

"What lie did you tell?" Asked William.

"I told them that you were working for the United States embassy in San Jose checking on Americans in the area." William tried to contain himself. That was not just a little lie. This was putting himself out there as a US employee. Also, a government official which could probably be either confirmed, or denied, by a simple check.

"I panicked and didn't know what to do," Regis said. William almost turned white but tried to remain calm. There was a way out of this. He just could not figure out what it was.

A moment later an officer came out of the back. He was the same man who had talked to Regis earlier. He walked up to William and started to ask him questions in Spanish. William looked at Regis as if to ask do you know what he is saying. Regis had been caught off guard and tried to cut into the conversation. He stopped the officer and informed him he would have to translate. The officer did not look pleased and said something while gesturing to William.

"What did he ask?" William asked Regis

"He was wondering why you work here, but don't speak Spanish."

"What did you tell him?"

"I told him you were new." William now thought that they were doomed. Everyone would really wonder why an American official would be sent to a country, and not speak its language. Either way they would have to just go with it. The officer continued to ask questions with Regis translating.

"Why are you here?" he asked.

"Tell him that I have information that an American is being held here, and that I have been sent to check on him." Regis did, and it only led to more questions.

"Under what authority do you ask this?"

"Any American citizen has the right to a representative of his government to assist him in his needs in this situation. I am acting under the guidelines of international law in regard to imprisoned persons, and treaties between our two nations regarding access to those charged with crimes," William answered making it all up. He went to law school and was sure there was something similar out there regarding the rights of prisoners. At least he thought there should be. The Officer looked around before answering. William's statements were making a dent, and he seemed reluctant to contradict what he was saying.

"He is asking why you don't have identification," Regis said.

"Our officers were told to not carry our credentials because of the recent risk of robbery of those documents. They are too valuable to just carry around in the present world environment." William knew that was a load of crap and hoped he would not be called out on it. Again, the Officer looked as though he wanted to say something but thought better of it. Without another word they were told to wait there, and the Officer disappeared again into the back. William had a strong desire to run but realized that being on an island in a foreign country did not help their odds of escape. It was time to just wait and hope it all worked.

The minutes seemed to go by very slowly. No one was particularly interested in what they were doing, and that bothered each of them. There had been no word on whether their ruse had worked. They stood there trying not to attract any attention, and also to not look guilty of anything. A few minutes went by, and the officer came back out. He walked right up to Regis and started talking. William waited until he was done and looked at Regis for an explanation.

"He says that you can go back and see that he is there, but there is to be no contact with any of the prisoners. They will allow you to look at where he is being held, and you will be able to view the prisoner to check his wellbeing."

"Tell him I am grateful, and that would be fine." William did not want to press his luck, and at least he would see that Chris is OK. They could then get the hell out of there and figure out what to do next. The officer started toward the back, and all of them followed."

"No" the officer said pointing at Regis and Marcus. Regis asked why he could not go as an interpreter but was told there would be no need. William was on his own.

"It's alright, I will be back in a couple of minutes," William told them as he disappeared into the holding area.

William did not like how this was going. He walked past guards watching a black and white TV. They took him down a long hallway toward a large metal door. When they got there the officer ordered it open. They moved through into a larger room with cells on either side. The place was not as bad as William had thought it would be and was much quieter. Men sat there looking at him as he walked passed. William searched for Chris but could not find him. At the end of the room was another door. Again they stopped it took a bit longer, but soon the door was open. William walked down another hallway into a smaller room with fewer cells. A slight man who was in prisoner clothing was mopping the floor near the door. The officer stopped William and pointed. Across the room William could barely see a man in a cell. It was Chris. By the looks of him he was fine, but William wanted a closer look.

"I need to see him closer," William motioned with his hands to try and get the officer to understand. However, the officer must have understood because he motioned no with his head and pointed to the ground as if to say stay here. William did not want to push his luck and tried to look like someone evaluating the situation. He moved a little and looked around the room. The Officer looked as though he was tiring of the situation. Again, he pointed to the floor, and then to William as if to say "stay here" and moved off.

He walked over to the cell and told Chris to stand up. Chris did so and looked up to see William. There was a puzzled look on his face as he saw his friend standing there. William did not move. He did not even want to show any sign of knowing Chris. They stood there for a minute looking at each other until William nodded toward the officer, and he moved away. He walked past William to another guard and said something to him.

The guard looked at William and remained seated. The officer then left the room. William knew the guard was there to make sure he did not move. There was no reason to try anything funny. He just wanted to leave. The guard would not take his eyes off William as he walked down the hall and sat down on a plastic chair. The slight man was near him with an old cart that looked like it was for cleaning. He would not look at William even though William tried to make eye contact a few times. The guard soon lost interest and went back to the magazine he had been reading. William put his head in his hands and wondered what he got himself into. Without realizing it the slight man had started to mop right in front of William.

"If you want to help you friend, you will find the leopard." William heard him say in an incredibly soft voice. Slowly, he lifted his head, and looked at the man. He was mopping without looking back at William. Chris had mentioned the Leopard in the letter, and here it was again. William looked away and waited for more. A small amount of time went by that seemed like hours to William. He was waiting for the man to speak again.

"You will find him here on the island," the man said. "Follow the path." With that he dropped a scrap of paper in a little ball at William's feet. He then mopped away from William blocking the view from the guard for a moment. William reached down and picked it up without alerting the Guard. He put it in his pants and remained seated without making eye contact with anyone in the room.

Almost a half an hour went by before another guard came through the door and motioned William to follow him. Without looking at Chris, he followed the guard out the door. William tried his best to not look like he was a fake smuggling information out of a jail. The hallways seemed a mile long on the way out. As the last door opened, he could see the waiting area. Resisting the urge to run as fast as he could to the exit, he walked over to where Marcus and Regis were.

"Well, I am satisfied with this trip," he said to them for no particular reason. They hesitated for a moment, and then realized that no one was keeping them there. William headed out the door with Regis and Marcus following. Not a word was spoken about what had happened inside the jail. The three moved off across the street as William tried to think of a place to stop and see what was on the paper. The town was awake and moving. The three got lost in the people coming and going. Moving down the street they finally found a small bar to tuck into and figure out their next move.

CHAPTER 16

William walked around the town a bit, stunned like a duck hit on the head. He had information in his pocket which could give some answers. However, he did not know where to go. He did not want to just sit down at a bar and look at it. There could be people watching. It was not like they did a great job with the whole US government act. For twenty minutes they walked around town. Neither Marcus, nor Regis, said a word. They followed behind William wondering what had happened inside, but too afraid to ask about it. They crossed paths with all of the different types of people wandering the streets.

Stalls were set out to serve fresh food, and vendors tried their hardest to put out their best sales pitch to the few people they thought could buy. All of it smelled wonderful, but they were too worried to stop so William ignored it all. Nowhere seemed to be safe enough to sit down. Every now and then they would pass a police officer. They tried their best to look like three tourists taking in the sights. Each time the officers ignored them. A bit of paranoia started to settle in. Every now and then Marcus or William would look around to see if anyone was watching them. Each time no one paid them any attention. If they were being watched, they would never know.

They started to enter a part of town that did not look the most welcoming. Marcus knew that sometimes looks could be deceiving. These parts of town sometimes only held poor people and were nothing more than a reflection of their economic circumstance. Consisting of good people working hard to make ends meet and wouldn't harm a soul. The people looked busy with very little concern for the new outsiders that were walking through their town. Besides, it did not look like a place that had a high opinion of the government.

"William, lets' just sit down and talk about this," Marcus said. William slowed his walked and stopped. Marcus saw a little shop selling food that had a couple of tables in front of it. He motioned over to it, and they sat down. For a moment everyone was quiet. Then Marcus spoke up.

"What happened in there?" Both he and Regis were starving for news about the minutes spent in the back.

"I saw him but didn't get to talk to him," William replied.

"Why didn't you talk to him?" Asked Regis.

"I didn't want to give anything away," William replied. "They were already suspicious of us in the first place. If I would have had contact with Chris, they would have found out that we were friends. Then we might have been right in there with him." Regis nodded that he had a good point. Chris was not in on it and would have blown the whole thing without knowing it. They got lucky.

"They wouldn't let me get close anyway," William continued. "I saw him from across the room for a few minutes. He looked alright. Probably a little confused as to why I was there, and just standing on the other side of the room."

"Did he say anything?"

"No, I guess he might have been too scared to speak up. He did not look hurt or anything. He just looked like a guy sitting in jail."

"Why the hell would he be in jail?" Marcus asked. "He never really would have taken chances that would get him locked up."

"We don't know what he was doing," said William. "Maybe it was being at the wrong place at the wrong time. Maybe he was involved in something that we don't know about."

"Why would you say that?" Marcus asked. William reached into his pocket and pulled out the small wad of paper. He held it in his hand without opening it. He did not know why he was so scared about what was on the paper. He set it on the table without unwrapping it.

"What is that?" asked Marcus.

"I don't know," replied William.

"What do you mean you don't know?" Marcus asked confused. "You just pulled it out of your pocket. Did Chris give that to you?"

"No, I never had any contact with Chris," William said. "Some guy just handed it to me."

"Someone just walked up to you and gave it to you."

"He was mopping the floor, and right before I left, he dropped this in front of me wanting me to pick it up." William picked up the paper again. He slowly unwrapped the paper. Marcus and Regis leaned over to see what was written on the paper.

"This is it," William said as a matter of fact.

The paper said: "*The Leopard. Go West. Pinaz town. Gingo. Old Man. Teacher. Find him. Answers. Your friend.*"

Somehow this guy knew of The Leopard. It seemed to be directions to find him on the island. At least now they had something to go on, and a way to get some answers.

"How did he know we were looking for The Leopard?" Regis asked.

"Who cares?" Said Marcus. "We need to get out of here and find out wherever he is."

William did not say anything. Obviously, Chris had hit on something that was a bit over his head. For the first time William wondered what it could be. He had always believed that Chris was in some trouble because of accident or misunderstanding. Now he started to wonder if there was something more. It could be that Chris had done something he was not supposed to do and is being punished for it. If that were the case, William did not want to push back very hard.

"Will, what are you thinking?" Marcus asked.

"Just wondering what to do from here," William replied. "The note names a town, which I guess is west of here. We need to figure out where it is and how to get there. Given the circumstances it probably would be best if we tried to keep a low profile. This island isn't that big, and we don't know a whole lot of why Chris is here." All of them agreed that is would be best to just lay low. They left the table and started to talk back into the city. They were going to find a place to stay for the night. Then they would look into where this Pinaz town was, and how they could get there.

Back in the holding area Chris sat in his cell puzzled. He just saw his old friend William standing there looking at him. He had not come over to check on him, or even said a word. Chris knew something had not gone as expected. He did not want to mess anything up by yelling at William to do something for him. Still, he wondered why William was there, and how he knew to come there in the first place. He hoped it had something to do with the letter he sent Marcus. At least he knew there were people around to help. The weight of helplessness felt heavier now. Chris knew that all he could do was sit and wait.

As darkness fell the slender man had finished his work and was taken back to his cell with Chris. Since his incarceration they had talked a little bit. Chris was happy that at least now he had someone to talk to, even if he was not much on conversation. The guard closed the door, and the two men waited for his steps to grow softer as he headed back to his station. No one was watched too closely, especially at night. They sat down and leaned up against the wall. Chris waited for the man to speak.

"Have friends stopped by to say hello?" He asked.

"I guess you could say that," Chris replied.

"Trustworthy friends?"

"As trustworthy as they come," Chris replied.

"I hope he will be able to help."

"If anyone can, it would be him," Chris replied. "Do you have anyone helping you get out of here?"

"I leave everything to others," the man replied. "I do what I can."

Chris pondered that statement for a moment. He did not really understand what the man was saying, but let it go. He did not want to give away too much information without knowing what William was doing, so he kept the rest to himself.

"Let us see if your friend can be any help to your situation," said the man as he laid down on the floor. "Maybe he can find a way to get you out of here." With that the man closed his eyes and tried to get some sleep.

CHAPTER 17

It had been a sleepless night for William. The small room they had rented above a bar was not what he considered five stars. In its best days maybe a two star, but it definitely was a one-star night. Not only did the sound from down below not die down until after 1:00am, but the thoughts of the day had not left his mind. Chris was obviously in much more trouble than William had thought. With their little stunt today, he and the guys could also have gotten into a lot of trouble.

When they got back, he, and Marcus, had talked about what Chris might have done. They went over all the things they could remember about Chris to see if they could piece together why he would be in this situation. Nothing they could remember would have led to this. There was no history of drugs or being involved with people he should not be. The thought of some sort of love triangle with a high-ranking officials daughter came to mind, but they thought better of it. Even though they doubted something sinister, they could not get it out of their head. William would not want to be helping someone the police put in jail for a good reason.

"Should we cut and run?" William asked. He did not want to, but he did want to know what everyone else thought about it.

"How could we do that?" Regis told him.

"We don't know why he is here," Marcus started. "But we can't just leave him here. I say we try and find the Leopard. We see what he can do. If all else fails, and we do not get anywhere, we can contact the US Embassy in San Jose. We can tell them Chris is here, and someone should look into it." William knew he was right. They could do their best, and if that did not work, turn it over to someone who may be able to do something. If it turned out that Chris did something wrong, there was nothing they could have done about it anyway.

After talking with Marcus, he tried to get some sleep. William lay in his bed as the town became quiet and thought about how to solve the problem. They were getting close to the Leopard, but he did not know what that meant. He hoped the next day would bring some answers. He looked down on the piece of paper he got in the jail. The town was Boma, and it was on the other side of the island. They had found a bus that made a round trip of the island every other day. It would be leaving the next morning and making a stop in Boma. There they would try and find the Leopard, and finally get some answers. William tossed, and turned, most of the night with the vague thought that any minute the police might knock down his door and arrest him.

Slowly the morning came upon the city. Animals were heard in the streets as vendors started to set up their wares. Sunlight fought against the drawn shade on the window. William had slept light and was easily wide awake at the first sounds. The other two were not so easily swayed from their slumber. The bus was to leave at 9:00 in the morning, but William knew that was not for certain. However, if they wanted to get started, they better get out of bed. William got up and looked out the window. The capital was also having a tough time waking up. It was a peaceful scene, and William stood in the window looking down at the street for a couple of minutes. Neither Marcus nor Regis had moved since he woke up. William shook Marcus' shoulder to wake him.

"Time to get going," he said.

"What time is the bus?" Marcus asked.

"It said around 9 o'clock, but hard telling what time it really leaves,"

"What time is it now?" Marcus said as he rolled over.

William looked at his watch. "6:45 a.m."

With that, Marcus made a noise and rolled over. William gave up the fight and decided to get something to eat. He grabbed his bag and headed out the door.

The best part of waking up in a small city was the activity of the morning. As William got to the street people were just starting to come out for the day. Thankfully, there were no McDonald's or Starbucks crowded with cars as the morning commuters started their day. Here it was fresh fruit, and coffee, from the local hills of the mainland for sale on the street. William started down the street stopping every few feet to look at the carts full of fruit for his morning breakfast. Coffee, tea, and some local beers were already being served in shops along the street. It reminded him of his days in Italy. He grabbed some local coffee, and a cup of fresh papaya. He sat down on a bench nearby, and watched the people go by.

Thankfully, when William got back to the room, the guys were up and almost ready.

"It looks good out there today," William said.

"Did you eat?" asked Regis.

"I just got done," William replied. "Just get something on the way to the bus station."

The bus stop was not very far from where they were staying, so there was no hurry. The guys picked up some fruit to carry along, Regis stopped to get a cup of coffee they had never heard of, and a few water bottles for the road. They did not know how long it would take to get to Boma, so they packed a few things to eat in case it was an all-day affair. The island was not that big, but given the nature of the transportation, no one could tell.

They made it to the stop with plenty of time on their hands. Marcus was able to get three tickets for a round trip with no problem.

"When does the bus leave?" Marcus asked.

"When it gets full," replied the ticket agent.

"When it that usually?"

"When it gets full," the ticket agent repeated.

Marcus walked back and sat down next to William.

"I guess we leave when they say we leave," he told them. "It could be in an hour, or tomorrow morning for all I know."

The guys sat down to watch the people make their way through the city. Given that they had just falsely put themselves out as United States Government representatives, and that they were all American, they stood out like a sore thumb. However, no one paid them any mind. Just another group of Gringos down for a vacation.

The bus pulled up only around 45 minutes late. The morning was getting hot, and by the looks of it there would be no air conditioner in their future. William, Marcus, and Regis climbed aboard, and took their seats. Their ride was a converted school bus painted bright green. The seats were more or less the same as they had been hauling school children, but there was little else for comfort. A few other passengers joined them, but many seats sat empty. Marcus found out the ticket agent was right when the passengers sat on the bus as a few people trickled in and took seats.

After another hour most of the seats were full. A man in a blue shirt, and jean shorts took the wheel. The bus pulled out along the bumpy road heading west out of town. The driver seemed like he knew how to navigate the town, but it was slow going. William knew it would take some time to get to the other side of the island. So he sat back, and watched the scenery go by.

Once outside of town it was a pleasant ride with the coast of the island to one side. The windows were down to give some refreshment from the heat. There were to be many stops along the way each adding time to the already long journey. The guys talked, and waited, as they bounced along the road at around 35 miles per hour.

The miles went slowly by as they made stop after stop at little towns along the way. After a few hours, the small town of Boma came into view. There was not much to it. A few ramshackle houses clustered along the road, surrounded by makeshift shops next to a dock. A medium sized boat floated at the dock. There was not much going on as they stepped off the boat. Certainly no welcoming committee comprised of an old gringo named the Leopard.

"Ok we're here now what do we do?" Asked Regis. Looking around there were not many options. William started to walk down the road toward what looked like a bar. When in need of information a bar would be as good as place as any to start. Besides, it was not a bad time for a drink.

"Let's just start asking people about an old ex-pat," William told them. "Certainly, if he is here people would know about it."

"Shouldn't we be a little more secretive about it" Regis asked. "I mean it's not like we didn't just see our friend in jail."

"I don't think the people here will give us a hard time," Marcus replied. "Hell, it took us hours just to get here. It would take hours to get word back to the police that we are out here." It did not look like anyone was about to run to the police and tell them they were there. In fact, there did not look to be any type of police around.

Even though there were only a handful of structures in the area, the guys found at least two bars within walking distance of the bus stop. The three guys dropped into their seats at the small bar by the dock. There was a lone bartender there watching a soccer game on a T.V. above the bar. He wore a soccer jersey, and there was soccer memorabilia on the walls, reminding William they were in a land of soccer fans.

"We don't see too many of you out here," he said coming over and standing in front of them. "What can I get you?"

"What do you have?" asked Marcus

"Not a lot," the bartender responded. "We have Imperial Beer, and a bit of hard stuff here or there that I could mix up." The thought of him just mixing something up did not appeal to William so he just asked for three Imperials.

"Sorry, only one of us speaks Spanish," William said, feeling as though an apology was in order each time he spoke.

"No problem. We speak more English than people realize," he replied. It was both an indictment of the United State education system, and the patronizing attitude of too many Americans. Most of Americans only know one language. The rest of the world knows at least two.

"So, what brings you to our great city?" He asked while wiping down the small bar.

"We are looking for someone," Marcus replied. "An older American who we were told might live around here. I guess kind of came down here for a retirement."

"Doesn't sound like a lot of people around here?" Said the bartender. "Here people just pass through. Not a lot of people stay. What you see is what you get." He made a gesture as though to say look around there are not many people here. "If you are looking for some older man from your country, I might be able to help you." The guys set down their drinks and suddenly were very interested in what he had to say.

"There is an old man that shows up every now and again in town," the bartender stated. "He has stopped by for a drink, but not very often. He will catch the bus over to the city and come back a couple of days later. He seems a bit off. Almost like there is something on his mind all of the time." The guys knew they were getting close.

"So where can we find him?" Asked Marcus.

"He is out on the island," the bartender replied. The guys sat speechless for a moment. All of them were thinking the same thing. They were already on an island.

"You mean he is somewhere on this island?" William asked.

"No there is another island," the bartender replied with a laugh. "That is what the boat is for." He pointed out toward the dock, and the lone boat bobbing in the water. "About twenty minutes west of here there is another island. Mainly for fisherman, but some crazies like to hang out there. I have only been there a few times; it can be a fun place. Sometimes a rough place, but a fun place."

"How do we get there?" William asked

"Just take the boat."

"Do you think we will find him over there?" Regis asked.

"That would be my guess," the bartender replied. The guys paid for the tab and headed toward the dock. The boat was manned by two men looking to be in their early twenties. They were told the boat only left twice a day, and the next one would not leave for about two hours. The guys decided to walk around the small town. The road led right through the middle of tin roofed shops and homes. The water of the Pacific was at the edge of town. William's Midwestern blood could never get enough of being by the water.

After a couple of hours, the boys boarded the boat with a few bleary-eyed fishermen that looked like they had been awake for two days. The crossing was bumpy, but thankfully uneventful. Few words were exchanged between the guys as they motored along the ocean. A sliver of land appeared in front of them, and they got their first look at *Isla sin Salida* as the locals called it. Regis asked if that was its official name. The boatman just said it had no official name.

"What does it mean?" William asked.

"Dead-end Island, I think," replied Regis. William did not think that was out of the question considering if they could not find answers here, they would be at a dead end.

The boat pulled up to the long dock to let off the few passengers. They walked down the dock onto a sand path leading into what seemed to be the town. There was not much there. The streets were sand, and there was no sense of organization. Once on the road they looked around to see if there were any places to go for information. Very quickly they found there was not. William saw a restaurant named the Sand Box to their right and figured it would be a good place to start.

The place was not busy when they walked in. Only a few patrons sat around the bar, and one at a table. For once everyone wanted to stay away from the bar. They were hungry from their long day and wanted something to eat.

"Well, I don't think you are from around here?" Said a nice lady who had come to the table.

"We are just visiting," Marcus said. She looked at him as if to say we already knew that. Even out in the middle of the ocean they spoke English.

"Do you have menus?" Regis asked.

"No, it's all up here," she said as she pointed to her head. "Out here it's pretty much just whatever we have around the place. That is what is on the menu."

"What do you have around the place?" William asked.

"I will bring you a grouper sandwich with our special hot sauce," she said. "I think you'll love it, and it is probably the best we have today. Then for dessert I will bring out ice cream, and chocolate syrup. Only place on the island you'll find it." She smiled as if to be enormously proud of that fact.

"Thank you that will be great," William said. "Don't mind me asking, but how do you know English so well living out here?"

"I was living in Texas for eight years honey before I came back," she said as she made her way back to the kitchen.

They were no closer to finding the Leopard sitting in the Sand Box, but the waitress was right, the sandwiches were great. There was nothing like fresh fish on an island. Even though William thought it funny, the ice cream was also good. Each of them got two scopes of vanilla ice cream in a bowl, and she set down a bottle of Hersey's chocolate syrup in the middle of the table. She told them to use as much as they wanted. William liked this island already.

As they were finishing up, she came back to the table. There were only a few other people in the place, and they were not giving her too much work.

"So why would the three of you come all the way out here?" She asked standing over them. It was like your mother asking why you were out so late.

"We're looking for someone?" Marcus replied.

"Nothing but trouble looking for people out here," she replied. "I must keep my eye out. You might be up to trouble." She sat down in a chair next to their table set on talking to them until she got the information she wanted.

"Who are you looking for, and why?" She asked.

"We're not exactly sure," William replied. "He is an old man from America. We were told he lived here, and we think he can help one of our friends." She looked at William, and then at the others.

"An old Gringo living on this island?" She said looking over at William.

"Yes, that is the last thing we heard," he replied. "We are at the end of the line, and don't know where else to go if he isn't here." She sat back in her chair shaking her head at all of them.

"It a long way to go to find some random old guy, but I think I can help." For the first time in a long time their spirits rose. This woman seemed to know who they were looking for. She treated them like she was helping an eight-year-old tie his shoes, but they did not care. As long as it led to the Leopard it was worth it.

"El Pirata!" The woman yelled to no one behind her.

"What did she say?" William asked Regis.

"She said pirate," he replied with a quizzical look on his face. William looked up and saw a man come in from the kitchen. All three of them held their collective breath as the man walked up to the table. Now he knew why she called him the pirate. He stood there is a white tank top, and red shorts. His head was shaved, but he had a goatee. In place of his left leg was a peg. William tried not to stare, but he could not help it. It raced through his mind that in modern medicine something surely could have been done to keep him from having a peg leg. To top it all off, he wore an eye patch. They sat there waiting for a parrot to pop out of nowhere and land on his shoulder.

William looked at Marcus, and Marcus looked at Regis. No one wanted to say a word. For a moment Marcus thought that they might be playing a joke on them. However, as they talked it did not seem to be much of a joke.

"He said he will take you to the old man," she said after her short conversation.

"Thank you." It was all Marcus could get out wondering how in the world they ended up on an island following a pirate to an old man's house. They paid their tab and left a little something extra for the help she gave them. The pirate was at the door waiting for them. William did not know what to do with him. He felt bad that this guy had to walk to wherever it was the old man lived. However, when they got outside the pirate pulled a bike up from the grass and got on. William looked down and saw that instead of where the left pedal would have been there was a ring of metal. His peg fit right in the hole.

"Made it myself," he said in Spanish with Regis translating.

They made their way slowly down the sand street. The island was not that big so William knew it could not be more than a mile or so. The pirate slowly pedaled his bike as the guys walked along side. The island did not have a town name or really anything that one would consider an organized area. There were places to eat, and buy stuff, but no real dining or shopping. As they made their way from the Sand Box they came upon a few houses. William was expecting for all of them to be ramshackle shacks on stilts but was surprised by the beauty of a few. More often than not the houses tended to be small but taken care of. There were no flower boxes or lawn ordainments, but clean and maintained properties. It was not too bad for a pirate town.

They walked with the sun behind them. The light had grown dimmer as the sun headed for the other side of the Earth. All of them were a little concerned about what would happen if he were not there or did not let them stay. At that point they had nowhere else to go. That concern fell by the wayside after ten minutes when the pirate stopped at a path leading back into palm trees next to a small house. It was probably the nicest looking house they had seen on the island. It was made out of mostly wood, with green painted sides, and a brown roof. The yard was nicely kept with palm trees framing each side of the house.

"You are here," the pirate said, pointing toward the house. With that he pedaled away back toward the town.

The three stood there for a moment trying to silently see who would be the first to go toward the door. Marcus broke the jam by starting to walk up the path to the house. The other two followed him up and stood behind him as he knocked on the door. A moment went by without any sound when suddenly the door swung open. Standing before them was a man who looked about 65 years old. He had white hair, and a grey beard. He wore blue shorts, and a tattered old shirt with a picture of a boat on it. He stood looking at them without saying a word.

"We are looking for someone," Marcus said. "He was a professor of History at the University of Kansas. Our friend Chris was in his class. He told us to come here." Marcus realized he was stumbling to find words. "He sent us to find you, or someone like you." The man stood there without saying a word. He studied them once or twice before he spoke up.

"I think you are looking for The Leopard," he told them. "And you have found him."

CHAPTER 18

The meeting was attended by a small group of people. That is the way the Colonel like it. The fewer people involved, the fewer reasons something could go wrong. However, nothing had gone wrong up to this point. They met just past midnight when the rest of the island was off to sleep. The people involved had known each other for quite some time. Their futures were now bound together. They met in order to finalize the taking of enormous amounts of money from the people of the island. It had been going on for over a year, and now was the time to cash in.

After the Colonel took power, he knew that it was to make money. His only concern at this point was making money. He liked the pomp and circumstance of being in power on the island, and he used it to his favor as much as possible. However, he knew he was at a dead end. He was ignored by the mainland politicians, as was the island itself. He knew that if he did too much, they would start to take an interest, and he would be out of a job, or worse.

Since the island was pretty much left up to its own devises, he hatched a plan. Tax revenue was taken from the people and handled on the island for the last twenty years. The thought behind this was that it took too much time and money to have it taken care of by the national government. If the island did not ask them for money, they could just keep the money they had. However, that meant there was very little oversight in regard to where the money would go.

For years, the government of the island were good stewards of the money. That changed with the Colonel. He saw an opportunity that he could not let go. Things had gone well over time, but there was always the chance of someone finding out. He had placed the right people in the right places but trusted none of them. Each of them had a reason to stab the next person in the back.

It started simply enough. He would work with a small team that included the head of the regional bank, and the head of the island treasury. This group could syphon off small amounts of incoming taxes and redistribute it to them. It had worked perfectly for the past year with more and more money being taken at a time. The Colonel was happy with his little nest egg. They were going to take a bit more and then slowly start to wind it down. In a few years they would leave the island and find a place to live out their lives with other people's money.

"This is going to be short," said the Colonel as he surveyed the group in front of him. "We need to find out how close we are to getting this done." His eyes shot to the head of the treasury for an answer. The man was small with a full head of hair that sometimes fell down on his face. Typical for a man that handles money he was dressed conservatively and would not look like a money launderer to the casual observer.

"We haven't reached our goal," he said as if giving a lecture. "The income is sufficiently proceeding. However, we need a few more months in order to get an amount we want." This statement was met by rolling of eyes.

"How many months?" asked the Colonel.

"I think we can do it in six months," he replied. The Colonel did not want to wait six months. He had held off the people long enough with stories of bad things waiting to harm them. He was running out of time, and things to use for fear. He knew the longer it went on the more time people had to ask questions. There needed to be an endgame.

"I give it three more months, and then cut it right there," said the man who headed the island bank. You could almost see that he was ready to take whatever was there and run. Everyone knew that he was more than happy to skim money and hide it in the bank. The Colonel suspected that he had been doing it before. Instead of arresting him, he brought him on board to help. He could not cut him loose now even though he wanted to. The idea of him taking the money and disappearing kept him up at night. The only solace was that the Colonel had him watched day and night to keep track of him. It was something he was keenly aware of, and one of the only reasons he stuck around.

The Colonel looked oddly disconnected from the conversation that was going on. He had wanted this to be over with but understood that it could not just end at the moment.

"Give it the time it needs," he said. "There is no need to rush it now. I will hold off on everything for a few months, and then we will start to make our exit." The exit had already been planned. After taking all of the money each of them would leave the island. First, there would be resignations. A few from the government, and a couple at the bank. The Colonel would stay until the end. The end being his sudden diagnosis of a serious illness. One that could possibly cost him his life. Once that was done, he would go seek treatment in several different places. All paid for by the good people of the island without their knowledge. He did not care where everyone else went, or what happened to them.

"How will we know when this is going to end?" the head of the bank asked impatiently.

"It will end when I say it is time to end," said the Colonel with a look that said do not cross me on this. Everyone knew he was not a man to cross. Each of them was anxious to get as far away from him as possible.

"In three months, we will be done," the Colonel said trying to ease the tension in the room. "At that time we will start the end game." He pulled a cigar out of his pocket, and an attendant came over to lite it for him. "It will not be long now."

CHAPTER 18

They stood in the entryway of a small, but well-kept, house of an old man. The kitchen was in front of them. It was small, but all one needed to support the cooking of a single person. The main room was off to the left. The furniture was sparse, but adequate. No one would have mistaken the place for one that did a lot of entertaining. However, none of the guys thought that is what the Leopard would do. The main room had a sofa, and a few chairs. In one corner there was a brown leather chair with a well- worn end table next to it. William thought it odd to have a leather chair on an island in the middle of nowhere. It looked like a good place to sit and read. Sitting and reading seemed to be the main use of the room. All around them were shelves of books. Stacks of books sat in the corner, and random books peeked out from nooks around the room.

As they walked into the room the Leopard sat on the leather chair and said nothing. He looked at them studying them without a sound. William walked slowly around the room looking at the titles of the books. It was a wide range of topics. He found Meditations from Marcus Aurelius, and various Hemingway books. Many of them he had never heard of. Meanwhile, the Leopard just sat, and looked. The house smelled of the island, mixed with the dust and untidiness of a single adult male.

Marcus and Regis sat on the couch trying not to look at the Leopard. All could feel his eyes looking at them, but none of them wanted to return a look. William did not mind. He was tired, and wanted to grab a book, and settle in and read until he fell asleep.

"Our friend is in jail," Regis blurted out. The room was silent after his statement, with William and Marcus looking at Regis as if to say, 'is that how you start things?'

"Is that how you really talk son?" asked the Leopard. "Do you have some sort of Turret's syndrome or you're about ready to crap your pants? I can't tell which one it is." He sat back in his chair and reached for a pack of cigarettes. Pulling one out, he lit it, and took a long drag before talking.

"Now you have come a very long way to sit in my living room and take up my time," he said. "Why don't you get to the point and tell me why you all are here." Marcus and Regis looked at William as if he were to be the spokesman of the group. William hated that he was the one who had to talk, but it looked like he had no choice.

"A few days ago, we got a letter from a friend." William started regretting that he had to even tell the story. He went through the whole thing. The whole while the Leopard sat looking out the window without saying a word. William did not even know if the story was getting through to him. He said Chris's name a few times hoping that it would strike a chord with the old man, but there was nothing. Finally, he got to the end where they came to his house with the pirate.

"So, that's about it," William said. The Leopard replied with more silence. All of them sat in the room listening to bird noises coming from outside. There was a bit of wind blowing against the house, and the light from the day was fading fast. In a few more minutes they would need to turn on a light just to see each other.

"Well, it's not the first time I have heard a story like that," the Leopard replied. He took another drag off his cigarette and put it out in an ashtray beside the chair.

"What do you want me to do about it?" The guys looked around at each other.

"Chris told us to go to you," Regis said. "We thought you would tell us what to do."

"So your friend gets into trouble, tells you to go to me, and I am supposed to just stop what I am doing and get him out of jail."

"Why would he tell us to go to you when he is in jail?" Marcus asked. "I mean he didn't have us contact the US government, or maybe his family. The letter said you."

"Maybe he didn't want the US government, or his family, to know what he was up to." William had not really thought about that, but it was a good point. His legal training told him that he should go to the US government first, because as everyone knows, they are here to help. However, law school does not give you any practical knowledge in regard to real life. Over the past couple of years real life has given him a few more lessons about how things are done. He knew the Leopard was on to something.

"So if he doesn't want anyone to know, then why does he go to you?" Marcus was pressing for something. "He couldn't have just picked your name out of a hat. He is in jail on an island not too far from here. He sends a letter halfway across the world telling us to get in touch with you. You happen to be just an island hop away from where he is. So there is something more to it." Marcus had hit it. The Leopard reached for another cigarette. As he lit it, and put it to his mouth, William thought he saw just a hint of a smile come across his face. The guys let the question hang out there in the room. Dusk had settled, and the room started to grow dark.

"You guys have had a long day," the Leopard finally said. "How about I take you out and get something to eat?" William's spirits started to rise. At least now something was going their way. The Leopard obviously knew more than he was letting on, and William's worry that they would be kicked out any minute had vanished.

"Drop your stuff here and follow me." It was an order immediately followed by all.

They headed out the door into the evening. The Leopard was wearing khaki pants with a hole in one knee and had put on a long-sleeved T-shirt. The guys did not have time to put anything on and headed out into the cooling air in shorts and shirts.

"I don't have many visitors," the Leopard said as they walked along the sandy path back to town. "That was the whole reason I moved out here. I wanted to get away from people."

"Didn't seem to work this time." Regis said.

"No, it didn't."

They walked along behind him tripping and stumbling down the path with no light. The Leopard did not seem to miss a step. William wondered how many times he had made this walk. It was enough to know all the bumps along the way.

"So how did you end up here?" William asked as they walked along.

"Well, it started a long time ago" the Leopard replied. "What is your name again anyway?"

"William"

"Well, Will it's a long story."

"It's William."

"Yes, Will, I heard you." There was going to be no arguing about it. William did not like to be called Will, but the Leopard did not like being told what to do. It was time to swallow pride and move along.

"I guess we've got time."

"Not as much time as it would take."

The group moved along until they came to the town. Darkness had fallen, and the shops were closing down. People were moving about the sandy streets. Heading off to find what little night life that must have existed on the island. The Leopard kept walking through the town, passing all of what looked like places to stop and eat. There was not much there to begin with, but when it was dark there looked to be even less. A couple of streetlights hung off of what were supposed to be light poles just off the sandy street. There were no sidewalks, and not much in the way of traffic. In fact, all William saw were a couple of modified golf carts moving up and down the street. In about two minutes the group made it past all of the ramshackle buildings that made up the town and were heading toward the other end of the island. The guys were getting tired considering they had been traveling all day, but the Leopard did not seem to mind. He just kept moving on.

"Where are we going?" Regis asked.

"I told you we are going to get something to eat" the Leopard replied.

"What do they have there?" Regis inquired.

"Mainly drinks" he said. "But I am told they could have some food too."

"Do you consider drinks something to eat?"

"If I need to, I do."

After getting out of the town the street was a street in name only. It became more of a wide sand path leading to the end of the island. Up ahead William could see a group of lights and thought that is where they must be going. The closer they came William saw that they had gotten to the end of the island. They had been walking for over 30 minutes. William was ready to sit down and have a drink. The place was an open-air bar that formed a hexagon, next to a gap in the island the locals called "the split". It looked to be well stocked with alcohol, but William did not see much in the way of food. It did not matter to him since he was not very hungry.

The Leopard sat down on one of the stools at the bar. Without a word the bartender sat a drink down in front of him.

"It looks like he has been here before," Marcus said.

"Probably on old pro," William replied. The guys sat down on the stools next to him. The bartender did not even acknowledge their presence. William, and the guys, knew well enough that there were many places were recognition was earned. The idea was to be patient and look like you belonged. Sooner or later you will get attention.

The Leopard sat looking over the split sipping on his drink. William could not tell what is was but could smell the alcohol a few feet away. At least they knew where he lived if they had to carry him home. William sat there, without a drink, and waited for the Leopard to say something. He looked around at the place. The seating was a few bar stools around the bar, and about half a dozen table scattered in the sand. On one side you could look out on the ocean, and the other was the split. It was not a bad place for a bar. There were about ten other people sitting around the bar, talking, and drinking. None of them gave William and the guys any notice.

"So, what do we do now?" Regis asked.

"Drink," replied the Leopard.

"What else?"

"What else to you do at a bar, son?" He replied. "Is this your first time at a bar?" The guys laughed knowing that there had been at least a thousand of bars before this one.

"Can you get these guys something to drink?" The Leopard asked the bartender. "Maybe with a few drinks they will be more enjoyable." That did the trick. In a matter of moments each of them had a drink in front of them. No one asked what they wanted, and none of them knew what they got, but it was not a time to ask questions. It was time to man up and drink the drink in front of you.

There was a cool breeze coming in off the water, and whatever the drink was, both were calming William. Not much had been said while the boys sat drinking. The Leopard would finish a drink, and soon the next one would show up. Every now and then the bartender would bring the guys something, and they would take it without questions. William sat there admiring the surroundings waiting for something to happen. He had hoped that a few drinks would loosen the Leopard up.

"How long is it going to take before you tell us why we are here?" William asked. He sat there looking at the Leopard seeing if there would be a response.

"I mean, you know something is going on, and you probably know why we are here. I can sit here all-night waiting. I have no other place to go. My friend is in jail, I am thousands of miles away from my girlfriend, and I would just like to know what the hell is going on." William did not want things to go downhill but thought he might as well put it out there. The Leopard sat for a moment. He finished off his drink and set it down on the table.

"Let's take a walk," he said. They all got up from the bar.

"No only him," he said pointing to William. Marcus and Regis looked at each other and turned to start another drink. William followed the Leopard out across the sand to the edge of the split. The Leopard lit up another cigarette and inhaled deeply.

"I knew this day was coming," he said. "I just didn't know it would happen like this." He never looked at William when he talked. He always seemed to fixate on a far-off object while talking.

"Your friend was a dumbass for getting thrown in jail. He should have never been that visible. I know he probably thought that since he was an American, they would never have tossed him in jail, but we now know that's wrong." William agreed with the harsh assessment of Chris but hoped that there would be a light at the end of the tunnel.

"There are a lot of people going to jail now. More than most people know. Chris came at just the right time we thought."

"What do you mean we?" William asked.

"There is more going on than just your friend going to jail," the Leopard replied. "We thought that Chris going to jail would be our big break. An American in this jail would shine some light on the island, and that would be enough."

"Why does light need to be on the island?"

"To tell you the truth I don't know really why it is happening. Things have been going downhill for a lot of people for a while now. People disappear and are not heard of for weeks or months."

"This is a bit more serious than I thought," William said

They stood looking out at the split and talked about the trouble on the island. The Leopard had been contacted months ago about helping the locals figure out what was going on. He, and a small group of people, had been working to find out what was behind it. They knew it was the government of the island and guessed that the mainland government was not involved. They had been gathering evidence, and stories, from people on the island. Now they were almost ready to take action. The sticking point was what action to take.

"Some people want to go through normal governmental channels," the Leopard told him. "But we do not know who is in on it, and how high it goes. Others want to just try and bring them down ourselves. Frankly, I am on that team. It speaks to the Revolutionary in me."

William was trying to take it all in as The Leopard went on. He had not been sure what Chris had been up to, but it was much more than he realized. The more the Leopard talked, the more William wanted another drink. He realized that he had not even been listening for a moment and had no idea what the Leopard had been saying.

"All right, I've had enough for right now." The Leopard stopped and looked at William. There had been a hint of anger in his voice, and it was shocking. William was mad. He was mad that Chris had gotten himself involved in the first place, and that he was there trying to put the pieces back together. All he wanted was to take a warm shower and get some sleep.

"I guess this is all a bit much right now," William told him. "Is there any way we can take a break, and pick this back up tomorrow?"

"Pick it up tomorrow?" The Leopard asked. "This isn't yard work Will, this is about people's lives." William did not answer, and just kept looking out over the water.

"We will need a day or two anyway," the Leopard finally said.

"What for?"

"We have to gather the troops." William did not like how that sounded, but he was not prepared to ask what it meant. He wanted to stop thinking about it for a little while.

The two went back to the bar and collected Marcus and Regis. The Leopard told them to head back and make themselves comfortable. He would be staying for a while. William guessed that it was the start of gathering the troops. On the way back, William explained what the Leopard had told him to Regis and Marcus. They had questions, but William did not have many answers.

"It seems that Chris is in a little over his head," Marcus said.

"I guess that is why he called us," William replied.

"I think I could like this," Marcus told him.

"Like what?"

"You know a jail break." William looked at Marcus seeing a smile come across his face. Only he would find the fun in the predicament they were facing.

CHAPTER 19

Quiza Bollo had been the head of the Island Bank for eight years. In that time, he had not made a single friend within the bank. He knew that he was over his head, and so did everyone else. Many wondered why the Colonel would tolerate a man like him. Quiza knew why, and he had been looking over the plan for the last 24 hours. It had only been three days since he had met with the Colonel, but things were now moving too fast for his own good.

He had been taking the government's money for some time now and planting it here and there to make a tidy profit for Colonel and the small group of swindlers. He liked to call them the investors. However, as the money grew so did the need to move it around to keep it hidden.

Things had gone far beyond his ability. The amount of money was too big, and the things that he needed to do to hide it were getting too complex. He needed to get out.

Quiza sat behind his desk as he had for the last six hours. He had arrived before first light and had not talked to anyone since the bank opened. The last report he saw at six in the morning showed that within days the money would be exposed. He had done his best to hide it, but there was no mistake now. Very soon it would be out in the open. Each of them knew the time would come when someone noticed the money was missing. However, they had worked it out so all of them would be somewhere else. He needed to tell the Colonel but did not know how. The Colonel was not a man who liked things to go wrong. Quiza had given the briefest of thoughts to just walking away with or without the money. His trip would not last long. The Colonel would find him, and he did not like the thought of what would happen next.

There were code words to describe the dealings going on with the Colonel. This was so they could talk on the phone or by correspondence without other people knowing. The phone sat only inches away, but Quiza could not bear the thought of picking it up and calling the Colonel. His office was always warm, but now it felt like the surface of the sun. Sweat stained his shirt as he looked at the phone. He knew what he was going to say. Things had to speed up. The money would be moved in the next couple of days. Each of them had an account where it would be deposited. That was the easy part. They then needed to move it again. That was up to each individual. They would then leave the island slowly over the course of the next year and enjoy their ill-gotten gains. Quiza thought he could go first. From the looks of him, no one would question if they were told he was ill.

Over the past few hours he had thought about what to do. If the money was moved now, and the group started to leave, it might work. There was a paper trail that would not take long to figure out, but all of them knew at some time the loss would be discovered. They hoped that by then they would be long gone on the other side of the world. There was risk to moving it earlier than they had planned, but he knew at this point they had no choice.

Pacing his office, he looked again at the phone. The more time he put it off the worse it would get. Soon it would be too late, and all of them would surely end up in jail. He locked his office door and closed the shade to cover the window. He had a direct line to the Colonel but did not even know if he would be there. *Not calling at this point would almost be worse than calling,* he thought.

With a shaky hand, he picked up the phone and dialed the number. After a few rings, a voice on the other end said it was the Colonel's office. Quiza told him who he was, and that he had urgent business with the Colonel. Lucky for him as the head of the Island Bank he could have access to the Colonel when needed. The Colonel's people knew if he called the Colonel wanted to talk to him. However, this still took time. He waited on the phone for minutes while the Colonel was found. Suddenly, a voice on the other end told him he was being transferred.

"What do you want?" Said the Colonel in a voice that sounded like it was not happy to be on the phone.

"The paintings are ready to be moved," He replied hoping the Colonel would be wise enough to remember the code words he used. The Colonel was silent for a moment on the other end.

"It's not time to the move the paintings," he stated in a calm voice. "I will call you and tell you when we need to move the paintings."

"Colonel, we have to move the paintings now," he stated emphatically. "They cannot wait." The Colonel started to understand that something had gone wrong. This was the one thing he knew he could not control, and it caused him to worry.

"Do not move anything until I come over and see the paintings myself," he told Quiza before slamming down the phone. He knew there was no turning back now. He was not ready to leave. He wanted a little more time to run the island as he wanted.

However, the trouble that was brewing would send them all to prison, and he knew his would be especially harsh.

He called his driver and made plans to go to the bank. His attendants set out one of his many uniforms to put on before he headed out the door. The Colonel was used to things going wrong every now and then, but even this had him a bit worried. Unusually, he put on his least abstentious uniform to make his appearance at the bank.

Plopping into his seat the Colonel settled in for the three-minute ride to the bank. The island was not that big, and the Colonel could have probably walked it in the same amount of time, but that was not his style. He would gather up everyone, and form a motorcade, to drive across the street. A few people stood on the street looking at the cars as they slowly made their way to the bank. The Colonel did not go to the bank very often, but as the head of the island government it was not something so unusual to cause much thought.

The door opened and the Colonel rammed his way inside. He greeted no one, except to salute no one in particular when he crossed the threshold. The people in the bank parted like the Red Sea when they saw him coming. Quiza's office was on the second floor, and he could feel the Colonel coming up the stairs to meet him. He sat in his chair looking at the door. The Colonel burst in with a couple of his goons nearby and sat down in a chair in front of Quiza.

"Leave us alone," he said without taking his eyes off Quiza. The two men with him slowly backed out of the room and shut the door. The Colonel looked at him for another moment, and then relaxed in his chair.

"What has gone wrong?" The Colonel said in a voice that hinted more of resignation rather than anger. Quiza let him in on all that had gone on in the past 24 hours. He told him where the money was, and why it needed to be moved. He explained the consequences of doing nothing, and how important it was to move quickly.

"How much time do we have?" The Colonel asked.

"A matter of days."

"How long will it take to move the money into the right places?"

"Not long," Quiza replied. "I have it set up so that the money can be moved in around 48 to 72 hours."

"Why not faster?"

"We can't move it all at once. That will trigger too many questions and will expose us to many risks. I would move it in bunches to different accounts. However, I need a couple of days."

"Do we have a couple of days?" The Colonel asked resigned to his fate.

"I think we do, but we have to act now," the Colonel got up from his chair and started to walk around the room. He knew there was no way around this. The plan would have to be executed now.

"Do any of the others know about this?" He asked.

"No, of course you are the first one I contacted."

"That was the right things to do," the Colonel said putting his hat on. "Start to move the money. Then you will notify the others. Get all of it out, and then shut it down. You will be taking a sick leave in four days. You have come down with a serious illness that needs treatment outside of the country. The others will spend the next couple of months getting their affairs in order, then it is up to them.

"What about you, Colonel?" Quiza asked. "What will you do?"

"I have always wondered about assassination attempts," he replied. "It would be a shame if someone tried to kill me in the next couple of weeks." With that, he left the office and pushed his way out of the bank. There was nothing to do now but wait. The Colonel started to dream up his next big act. A farewell that would leave him in the mind of the people forever.

CHAPTER 20

The guys got to spend a couple of days hanging around the island. The Leopard had told them it would take a few days in order to get everyone together. He did not explain who these people were, or why they needed to get together, but the guys just took it in stride. William spent his days walking around the island. He could pretty much circumnavigate the whole thing in less than a day. In the morning he would wake himself up with a Mojito in the morning to get things going. It was hard to get coffee this far out the Leopard had told them, so alcohol was the next best thing.

The Leopard was no stranger to the same morning ritual, so when in Rome. He awoke early to see the island at dawn. In the small town the fishermen were readying their small boats for the day. It was like a scene from a story from long ago. The men sat on stones just off the water, bantering in low voiced Spanish while mending their nets. They were hard at work, but not in a hurried way, or in a way that would show the difficult work that lay ahead. He'd heard there had once been many fishermen that came out to the island. Now there were only a handful. It was an awfully hard way to make a living.

As he walked around town William would randomly run into a local. He would put on a friendly smile and say Hola. Most just nodded, and a few ignored him completely. He guessed it was the same around the world. People were not always unfriendly, but just wrapped up in their own little world. What William liked the most was being by the sea. William liked the salt smell of the air. It reminded him of living on the coast of Italy. Sometimes he would walk back up to the split and take a swim. There the water was protected on each side so there were no waves. The bar had closed a few hours before, so there were no people. After he was done, he would walk back outside of town on the West side of the island. It was rough, but one could make it if they went slow.

William would meet up with Regis and Marcus in the late morning. The Leopard would come in and out without saying what he was doing or where he was going. They figured he would tell them when they needed to know. The guys would go into town for a bit, and maybe get another drink, before starting their lazy afternoon. A few days of this would be fine, but the guys were itching to get something done about Chris. The Leopard told them to wait. This type of game took time to develop. He told them that things were coming together to help Chris. It would not be long now. So they waited.

The Leopard had been up to something. The guys would see him leave in the morning, come back for a bit, and then leave again. He told them they could not go along where he was going. They were told that he would let them in on what was going on soon. There was no attempt to argue.

Since the Leopard would leave them in his house for long periods of time, William took the time to look around. He knew truly little about the Leopard, and he was not getting much of a backstory when he asked. William poked around bookshelves, and in drawers. A twinge of guilty would pass over him as he knowingly snooped around. However, since he was trusting this man with his freedom it seemed a fair trade.

As he sat flipping through a book an old picture fell out. It was a young man in an army uniform standing with other young guys at what looked like an air base. There were four of them looking a bit young and Marcus and Regis. Their arms were around each other smiling at the camera. Names were written above three of the men. William could only assume the fourth was the Leopard. He put the picture back in the book and returned the book to the shelf. There were lines of books on politics, history, and philosophy. The hard stuff that no one really wants to read but tries.

Little trinkets from around South America dotted the desk as he sat down. A bright green plaster salamander looked at him as he opened a drawer. It was full of old newspaper clips, and an assortment of names and dates on small pieces of paper. As William took the paperwork out of the drawer, he saw something strange at the bottom. A green file with the word "smarts" handwritten on the front of it. When he opened the file, he saw a Diploma for a Ph. D in Philosophy. It had been deliberately marked on. However, the main part stating the Degree confirmed was still legible.

"So we are dealing with a doctor," William said to himself as he slipped the file back into the drawer. He sat there alone pondering what to make of their strange host. What was he to make of a veteran with a Ph. D hiding out on a remote island? Not knowing the answer, he decided to keep it to himself for a while.

Time moved slowly on the island. Having a friend in jail, and waiting on answers, made it slower. As evening settled in after three days of waiting the Leopard came through the door to find all three guys laying around the room. There was no TV just a small radio that got almost no reception, and a lot of books.

It was not a lot to hold the attention of three young men. They three friends had talked over everything time and time again. There was no interest in talking about it again. Just waiting to be told what to do next.

"I see you are using your time wisely," he said as he grabbed a drink from the kitchen. There was no response. Each of them knew this was just the way the Leopard interacted with them. They could take it.

"Just waiting around for something to happen," Marcus said. "Still just waiting around."

"Well, something is about to happen," he replied. "So, you might want to get off your ass and look presentable." All three perked up and looked at The Leopard.

"What is going to happen?" Regis asked.

"We are going to have a little meeting here tonight," he said. "It took me a couple of days, but I think I have the whole gang coming out here tonight."

"Who is coming out here tonight?" William asked.

"It's not like you would know any of them if I told you." It was a good point, and William let it go. At least something was going to happen. He hoped they would have some idea of what to do about Chris.

"Sir," Regis said. "I don't really want to get mixed up in anything bigger than what we already have. I mean it seems like Chris is in enough trouble already."

"Too late, son," replied the Leopard. "You came all this way to get involved in something bigger. So, you are here now, and you're in it whether you like it or not." It was more of a command then anything. If any of them had a thought of trying to get out now, it had been dashed rather harshly. William figured they had come this far, what could be any worse.

"What is this meeting for?" Marcus asked.

"To plan our course of action," replied the Leopard as he sat in his favorite chair and lit a cigarette.

"When will they be here?" William asked.

"I don't know," he replied. "They will get here sometime tonight, and then we will start. Until then we will find some food and have a drink."

"Shouldn't we have a clear head if we are going to plan something important?" Regis asked naively.

"Son, I can't have a clear head without a drink," rhe Leopard replied. "And given what you are about to get involved in, I would advise a drink or two before we start." That did not make any of them feel better.

They made their way back to the bar at the split for a drink, and a bite of food. The walk did them some good. Marcus and William let The Leopard and Regis walk ahead of them so they could talk.

"I don't know if I like what we are getting into," William said.

"I knew you wouldn't, but I don't think we have much of a choice at this point," Marcus replied.

"We don't know what they are doing, or who is involved."

"Yea, but Chris sent us here, so he must have thought this was the best way to take care of things. I don't think we would have led us to the Leopard if he didn't think it would help." William was not surprised that Marcus like where this was heading. It was his adventurous spirit that allowed him to be comfortable in these situations. It was not the same for William.

"We just needed to make sure to watch out for each other," William said.

"Agreed."

A short while later they sat at the same places and ordered drinks. There was little conversation. The guys did not feel in the mood to talk, and the Leopard did not care to. William sipped at his drink, Marcus finished off his, and Regis order two more. None of them wanted food before the meeting. The days seemed to last forever to William. It was time to get something done, and he was growing tired of sitting around waiting. Thankfully, the Leopard stood up, and said it was time to head back.

"It's time for the meeting to start," he said, making his way back toward home.

"How do you know?" Regis said with a slight slur.

"I just know," he replied. "They will be there now." William and Marcus followed behind him hoping he was right. Darkness fell with a quickness they were not used to coming from high Latitudes. Twilight is short, and darkness comes early. The air cooled as they made their way back to The Leopard's house. As they came closer, they could tell someone was in the house.

"Did you tell them they could just come in and hang out?" Marcus asked.

"No, but it wouldn't have matter if I told them not to either," the Leopard replied.

"Must be some close friends," William said.

"Who said these were friends," the Leopard shot back. The statement did not make William feel any better about their upcoming meeting.

The Leopard walked through the door to find about a half dozen people around his main room. Several conversations were going on at one time. All of them in Spanish so William had no idea what anyone of them were talking about. Once the guys stepped into the room all conversation stopped. Some eyed looked toward them, but others looked away. William heard The Leopard say something in Spanish, but he did not know what.

"Regis, you'll have to keep close to us so we can figure out what they are saying," William told him.

Two of the men huddled with The Leopard speaking in hushed tones so not even Regis could make out what they were saying. Soon everyone except the guys were in a small circle talking. William did not know if they were supposed to join in, sit down, and go home. They decided it would be best to stay where they were and wait. Minutes went by with the group still huddled talking.

"Regis, go over there and figure out what is going on," Marcus said.

"I don't want to go over there," he replied. Marcus gave him a push that sent him halfway across the room. He slowly moved closer, so he was within earshot. No one noticed, or cared, that he came over. The conversation was getting a bit louder now, but William still could not make out what was going on. Strong hand gestures were being made, and it sounded like there were some serious disagreements being hashed out.

The men began to settle down and took seats around the room. Regis came over to where Marcus and William were sitting. The Leopard got up and started to talk to the group.

"You are going to have to translate for us," Marcus said to Regis.

"Just keep quiet, and I will try and figure out what they are saying," he replied. Regis told them that he was asking them to take action now. They had waited too long, and too many of them had been taken away. It was only a matter of time before more of them would be found.

William could tell that Regis was paraphrasing, but it was the best he could do. Another man stood up and started talking. He said that everything was in place, and that the information from the inside said that it was time. He went on to say they could use the Americans as a diversion.

"What diversion?" William asked in English to the whole group. Regis translated quickly, and the man replied in a lengthy retort with more hand gesturing. Regis did not translate until he was all done.

"He said they need someone to go in and distract the guards for a time. None of them could do it because they would just be taken into jail. They think that since we are Americans the guards will at least pay some attention to us, and then they the can do their work." William did not like how that sounded.

"How does this get Chris out?" Marcus asked. They had to wait for a translation, and then a reply.

"They said they are getting everyone out," Regis told them.

"What do you mean?" William asked.

"A jail break son," said the Leopard. "We've got their get out of jail free card." William sat back in his chair and could not believe what they had gotten themselves into.

"I'm going to kick Chris's ass when we get him out," he said to himself.

"So how exactly are we going to get him out?" Marcus asked. The Leopard looked at one of the men in the room who waited for a second, and then seemed to give the go ahead to tell them.

"Frankly, we are just going to blow a big damn hole in the wall and let everyone run out," he said. William waited for more, but there was no more to come.

"That's it?" William asked.

"Yes, that's it," the Leopard replied. He got out another cigarette and lit up. There was no hint at a need to say more.

"Don't you think that is a bit simple?" William asked. The Leopard looked at him with a look of annoyance. He did not reply, but exhaled a cloud of smoke, and took a drink.

"What part do we play in this?" Marcus asked trying to get some more information.

"Now that's more like it." said the Leopard. "You guys are going to go in and ask some questions. Make some noise, and demand to see the American. Do whatever it is young people from our country do to get attention,"

"What are you guys going to do while we get attention?" William asked.

"We are going to blow a big damn hole in the side of the wall," the Leopard said while slowly making his way over to where William was sitting. "Then after the big damn hole is blown in the wall, the people inside will be able to run out of the big damn hole. Once they run out of the big damn hole, we will pick them up, and get them out of there," he finished, standing over William and smoking his cigarette. There did not seem to be any sense in arguing about it.

"How are we going to blow a big damn hole in the wall?" William asked resigned to the task at hand.

"Oh, we have a man for that," the Leopard replied. "I think you have met him."

"When did we meet him?" Marcus asked.

"He is the one who led you to my house." Marcus looked at William, and Regis. The pirate was in on it also.

"You mean the guy with one leg is an explosive expert?" Regis asked.

"I didn't say expert," the Leopard replied. "Why do you think he only has one leg?" That did not make any of them feel better. However, the deed was done.

"When do we go?" William asked.

"48 hour from now," the Leopard replied.

William and Marcus left the meeting and took seats outside. Marcus had brought a couple of beers, and they sat in silence in the cool night air. Regis had stayed inside to listen to the plans they were making. He would come out later, and fill them in. William had a hundred question about what was going to happen. He was a planner and did not like the idea of just following along with someone else's plan. This would be his last chance to get out. It was the kind of choice that was make or break in how the next part of life would turn out. It also said a lot about a person, and who they would stick their neck out for in life. He sat there and thought of Maria, and how much he loved her. He thought about how it would feel going back to her without following through with his friends. As much as he wanted to leave to get back to her, he knew that he would stay. Looking at Marcus he knew he could not leave his friends. Marcus would stay, and if Marcus stayed so would Regis. William could not leave them to save his own skin.

"Here is to another adventure," William said as he touched beers with Marcus.

"Does that mean you are in?" he asked.

"I'm in."

CHAPTER 21

The night had been a long one for William. After about an hour Regis came out of the house to talk to the guys. The plan was done. There were a few things that Regis did not understand, but he got most of it. He had told them about how they had already gotten inside the jail the first time. It was decided that it could work at least one more time. They would go in and demand to see Chris again, saying they had information from the United States Government that they needed to give him.

Most of the people on that shift would not understand what to do with that information. It really did not matter how far they got, only that they needed to bring as many guards to the front as possible. That will give the others a chance to get into position without being noticed. While the guys were inside, the others will blow the crap out of one of the walls. Once all hell breaks loose, everyone was to get the hell out, and make their way out of town. From that point on each was on their own until they got back to the island. There they already had places to go for everyone to lay low.

"What about us, where do we go?" asked Regis.

"We are coming back here. No one seems to think they will put up too much of a fight for Americans," Replied William.

"Won't blowing up a jail bring in a lot of outside help for them?" Marcus asked. "I mean we are going to commit a pretty serious crime."

"That is what they said they wanted," Regis replied. "Once word gets out the mainland government will be out here in a second. They won't have any choice."

"How will that make it any better?"

"They keep saying that once the mainland government gets out here things will become clear. Something about the people in jail are not supposed to be there, and a big amount of money is missing."

William had his doubts things would work as smoothly as they were talking. However, he did not have any better ideas. Now he just wanted to get it over with.

The little party had dispersed late in the night to start preparations for the next day. There was nothing for the guys to do other than wait. Their part would be small, and mainly just a re-enactment of what they had done just a few days prior. The plan seemed to be too simplistic and did not take into account the prospect of someone being hurt or killed. No one other than William seemed to care. So, it went on. William waited to play his part and hoped like hell things would turn out fine.

The only thing William did not like more than the part he had to play, was that he had a small part to play. The Leopard was busy talking to the people involved and running in and out of the house. He seemed almost giddy that he had something sinister planned. Marcus was content being on the inside of a daring plan that would give him a little bit of adventure. Regis was trying to hold himself together for his part by downing cocktails. He would again have to go inside the lion's den and help translate for William.

Bit by bit people and things started to trickle into The Leopard's homestead. Since there would be around 12 people involved, plus all of the things they would need to bring, not all of it could happen on the island. The Leopard would periodically update them on each new piece of the puzzle that would come together.

"The trucks have arrived on the main island," he would say in passing. "The transport is there." All William could muster was a nod, or a shrug. The Pirate had come by a couple of times to talk to the Leopard and looked downright excited to be on board. Given his experience with explosives William questioned whether he would be a good choice. For good or bad, he quickly had assembled a cache of explosives. Many of which William could not recognize even as they were laid out in the middle of the room in the Leopard's house. Marcus was another who could hardly contain his excitement. He would sit and talk to The Leopard about the plan and would help the Pirate unload his boxes of explosives.

"You have got to be more upbeat about this," he would tell William. "For better or worse, we are in this, and we are doing it for a good reason." William knew he was right but could not shake the nagging feeling that there was a better way to go about it.

"I just don't like how it is all happening," replied William.

"You never like how it is happening because everything moves too fast for you," Marcus said. "Sometimes we don't have a month to sit around and think about what to do. Sometimes you just have to take action. Come on William. Less thinking, and more action." He finished by knocking his hand on William's head before he walked away. William also had a hard time understanding Marcus' optimism about things. If he found something he believed in, he would jump in with both feet.

There would be one more night before the team would head out. Everyone had planned to go to The Split, but William was unsure.

"You have got to stop sitting here, and pouting," said Marcus.

"Yeah, come with us so we can go out with a bang," Regis said. Marcus and William looked at him with concern for his choice of words. "Sorry, I didn't mean it like that."

"We need to talk one more time about what we are going to do tomorrow," Marcus said. "We need you there to go over things." William decided to relent. If they had to go through with these plans, then it would be a good idea to go over them one more time.

The others had set out ahead of the guys in the darkness. Night had fallen, and William had for the first time put on another layer of clothing to ward off the coolness. There was not much more to talk about as they made their way to The Split. They were coming to the end of the journey for good or bad. Mainly, it seemed, they just wanted to get through the next day. Walking up to the bar they found festivities in high gear. There were probably around 30 people crowded around the bar, with The Leopard at the center, smoking and drinking as usual. The guys found chairs a little way away from the bar and sent Regis to grab a few drinks.

"What do you think about getting Chris out?" Marcus asked.

"I don't think it will work, and we are going to end up in there with him," William replied. Marcus shook his head as Regis came back with the drinks.

"Have a little faith man," Marcus said as he took a drink. "Things will be all right."

"I am just ready to get out of here," William said.

"Have to talk to Maria?" Marcus asked.

"I e-mailed her a couple of time since we took off," William replied. "I left it kind of vague considering what we are doing. She knows us so she didn't ask many questions."

"Is that your girlfriend?" Regis asked.

"Yes, and I hope to keep her around," William said looking at Marcus. "So how about we stay home for a while so I can see my girlfriend."

"Agreed, no more running off."

The drinks did help. Since they were going to participate in a jail break the next day, their nerves were on edge. William was especially concerned. He did not want to let on too much that he was scared to even go through with it. However, he thought of Chris sitting in a cell, and wanted to do whatever he could to get him out. If this was it, then it needed to be done. The first drink was done, and then so was a second. William knew they should talk then before they were unable.

"So, are we ready to go in?" William asked.

"We're ready," Marcus said. "But I know you want to go over it again so give it a shot." He was right William just wanted to go over it one more time before they left the next day.

"One more time," he said.

Their part of the plan was not too complicated. They were to go in and cause a scene to draw as many guards to the front as possible. The others were going to be stationed around the building to blow certain parts of it apart. They had said that they had taken into consideration where guards and inmates would be at the time so no one would be hurt. William had wondered how they could do that and was told they would have help from the inside. Once the scene had started there would be two different blows. One would be toward the front to close access to the holding portion of the jail. Once closed off another would be to blow a hole in the side to get everyone out. If all worked out as planned most of the guards would be up front to deal with William, Marcus, and Regis. From there they would not be able to do anything about what was going on behind them. The only real question mark in William's mind was how they were supposed to get out when everything started to blow up. That really was not dealt with, other than The Leopards telling them to do their best.

"That is about it," William said as he picked up his glass. The guys were silent for a moment as they took in their responsibility one last time.

"I guess there is only one thing left to do now," Marcus told them.

"What is that?" William asked.

"Get drunk," he said as he walked up to the bar. Regis looked at William and smiled. William thought if it could be his last day of freedom for a while he might as well have some fun. Marcus brought over a shot for each of them, followed by another beer. They were dispatched quickly and replaced by another round. For a brief moment The Leopard came over and saw that they were well on their way to having fun, and decided he was too old to try and keep up. William was correct in having his conversation with them early, because soon none of them were in any mind to talk.

"Regis, it is your turn to get drinks," Marcus said with his head bobbling up and down.

"Get what?" Regis said staring off across the water.

"Drinks."

"Drinks?" He replied again.

"Yes, drinks," Marcus told him. "It starts with the letter d."

"What is a d?" Regis said laughing

"It's a consonant," William stated.

"Consonants…I know what those are. They are the r's and s's of the alphabet," Regis said confidently. He stood up and made his way to the bar crashing into almost every person he saw. William watched his friend crash his way to the bar for one more round. He knew they should start to make their way back, or soon they would not be able to make it back at all. He was still worried about what lay ahead, but the drinks had done their work. Now he was simply happy to have the opportunity to sit with friends and have a little fun. The night would be left at that.

CHAPTER 22

It had been lights out for almost 30 minutes before he spoke up. Chris and he had been cell mates for days now, and a bit of trust had built up between them. Now it was time to let him in on a secret. The only time they could talk was at night. During the day there were many jobs to do around the jail, and many prying eyes, and ears, to interfere. It had been days since Chris saw his friends, and he was still wondering why they had shown up. He had not told his cellmate about who had come to visit him. Each day he hoped they would do something to get him out of jail.

"You should know that something is about to happen," said the slender man who shared his cell.

"What is about to happen?" Chris said, getting up from his bed to hear. Nothing much went on inside a jail, so the news of something happening was a welcome surprise.

"I have some friends coming to get us."

"What do you mean coming to get us?" Chris asked.

"My friends have been working for some time to figure out a way to get us out of here," he stated. "Many months ago, friends of ours were taken away. We did not know where they were, or if they were coming back. I found out they were in here, so we started to plan." Chris sat down in surprise that his warry cell mate was really a mastermind escapist.

"Plan what?" Chris asked. "What are you talking about?"

"I am talking about how we will not be here after tomorrow night." He paused to look out the cell to see if anyone was around. Not surprisingly, there were no guards around let alone someone who would pay too much attention to anything. It reminded Chris of the line from Count of Monte Cristo that said neglect is our ally.

"My friends have found a way to get us out. You, and your friends, have provided us with an opportunity to get out tomorrow." Chris was speechless. Not only was he talking about getting out of jail, but he was also talking about his friends.

"How do you know my friends?" Chris asked.

"I know a lot more than you think," he replied. "I saw him come in here. I knew that he was someone close. He has made contact with my friends on the outside, and it is almost time."

"Almost time for what?"

"To go home."

Chris was confused. He did not understand how his friends could have gotten involved with men his cellmate knew. All he could do was keep asking questions. The only answers he got were that they were going to get out the next day, and his friends were in on it.

"Could you just start from the beginning and tell me what is going on," Chris said to him.

"Fine, sit down and I will tell you how we got to this point."

The slender man came down from his bed, and he and Chris sat on the floor. He started from the beginning. Months ago, friends of his started to disappear. It was only one or two at first, but this was a small island, and everyone knew almost everyone else. Some thought that is was just men striking out on their own over on the mainland. It was not unheard of to see someone go off to make their way where there was more opportunity. However, more started to disappear.

Shortly after that, some started to come back. They did not want to talk about what happened to them but were obviously shaken. Once they would talk, they would described being grabbed by police and taken to jail. There they would be held for weeks without knowing why. Every now and then they would be brought before the guards, beaten and questioned about others. Even when released, they knew not to talk about what went on. They were told to stay out of State business or risk returning.

So, the warning went out. Stay out of the way or be taken out of the way. It did not stop there. More were taken, until he could not stand any more. He and a small group of friends started to meet in secret. They watched the police, and the government in general. They were beginning to have help from the inside, but things got out of hand.

People started to talk, and meet out in the open, thinking they would make more of a difference. His group knew that only way in which to stop the government was to have someone on the inside of the jail to see what was going on. That is why he allowed himself to be seen at the meetings. He knew he would be reported, and taken in. That is why he was out in the open. The only question in his mind was Chris.

"Why would you get involved?" He asked.

"I just wanted to help in any way I could," Chris said. "I could tell something was going on. That something was wrong. I didn't understand the stakes of the game and got caught." There was a bit of silence before the slender man spoke again.

"It was a benefit to us that you are here," he said. He explained how his friends were going to help in the jail break. There were not any specifics, and Chris could not tell whether he was just keeping it from him or did not know himself.

"They will be here tomorrow night," he said. "It will be our job to get as many guards away from the walls as possible."

"How do we do that?" Chris asked.

"Easy, we do the work for them," The slender man went on to say that there were jobs the guards were supposed to do but would gladly let the prisoners do. Mainly, it was cleaning the area around where they worked. It would be Chris's job to get one of the sentry guards overlooking the wall to leave so Chris could clean his station. The slender man would do the same for the sentry guard at the other end of the wall. The rest would be left up to their friends.

Chris was left contemplating the fate of him and his friends. The slender man had gone back to bed as if nothing were amiss. Chris could not sleep. The thought of the whole thing failing, and his friends ending up in jail with him repeatedly crossed his mind. He wondered how his cell mate knew these people, and how he got all of the information.

For a moment Chris wondered whether it was a trap set up by the guards to see if anyone was trying to escape. He looked up at his cell mate, who was already asleep, and wondered where to put his trust. He was getting tired of jail and had almost reached out to his family for help. That is the last thing he wanted to do.

In the back of his mind he was worried about having to explain exactly what he was doing down there. The truth may not set him free in this case. He knew his best chance to get out without having to let anyone else in on where he was lay with his friends. He had seen William come to the jail so what his cell mate was saying had a hint of truth to it.

He climbed back in bed wondering how he would do his part. A hundred questions raced through his mind as he thought about the day ahead. He had no idea how they were going to get out, and what they were to do once they did get out. However, it was set now. He thought about his friends and how The Leopard must be involved somehow. It was only fitting that it would end like this. A scenario that only The Leopard would be involved in.

CHAPTER 23

A meeting had been called for a small group of men who were about to be extraordinarily rich. It was late at night, and the bank had been closed for hours. It was not usual for the bank President to work late after many of the other had gone home. He had almost lived there for the past few days. Only a handful of people were there, and all were excited to hear what he had to say. However, the meeting could not start until the most important player had arrived. The Colonel would be there on his own time. The other could just sit around and wait. A few of them whispered to each other about how much money would come their way. The plan had been put in place for years, and now was the time for the payout.

An hour after the others had arrived the Colonel walked in. This time there was no entourage with him. He had left only one-man downstairs, and a driver in the car. There was no need for him to tell anyone where he was going. He went wherever he wanted without question. A seat at the front had been arraigned for him. He took his seat without a word being said. The Colonel took off his hat showing his balding head. The hat was set down on the floor beside him, as he looked up at the bank president.

The bank president looked like he was about ready to teach a class at a high school. The sleep deprivation had taken its toll. He looked like hell. However, he did manage to pull off the transfer of millions of dollars in assets in a little over 48 hours. No one was more surprised than himself.

"This is a little ahead of schedule, but we had no choice." he stated. "I have been able to collect 12 million dollars in the accounts specified by our earlier agreement. This will be the only time that I issue paperwork in regard to the amounts each will receive," With that each of them was handed a piece of paper. On it was an account number, and the amount of money in the account. At the bottom of the page was a date.

"You will see that each of you have an account here at the bank. The amount of money in that account is the amount you agreed to when we started this endeavor. That is yours to take and execute the withdraw plan. The date at the bottom is the date the funds will be ready for withdraw or transfer,"

Each of them looked down at their sheet of paper. The dates were done by who was the most important. The Colonel's date was the next day so he could have access to his money as soon as possible. Whatever it was he would do at that point did not involve the rest of them. The others had dates staggered over the next couple of months. The amount of money in each account was tantalizing. However, they had to wait to open their presents. They knew the Colonel would go first and did not dare challenge him. They would wait and take their stolen money in due time.

Only one person had already taken his money. The Bank President could not wait. He did not trust the Colonel and was worried something would go wrong. Quietly, he had transferred his money earlier in the day. It was spread out in a few different accounts in three different countries. Soon he would take his leave and visit each of those countries to pick up his stash. He decided to keep this to himself. He also had a piece of paper in his hands. He made sure the Colonel, who was seated right in front of him, could see that the date on his paper was two weeks away.

"What happens if someone finds out about this before the money is moved?" Said one of the men.

"It is imperative that no one touches the money before their date," the Bank President replied. "It is too much money for this institution to have and will tip off authorities on the mainland. Once the money is moved, I will cover the tracks here at the bank." That was a lie. He had no intention of covering anyone's track but his own, and that had already been set in motion. He would be gone, and everyone else would be left on their own. He did not care if they made it or not.

The Colonel stood up to address the gathering. As always, he wore a military uniform that was heavy with assortments of medals and ribbons.

"We have a plan in place that will benefit each of us," He started off in his prepared speech to the group.

"Each of us has an obligation to do their part. If we all do what we have promised to do, then everything will turn out fine. This is the last time we meet. Now it is up to each of us to part ways and live long prosperous lives." It was not a stunning speech, but the Colonel felt the need to make the address. He never wanted to see any of these people again and did not care one bit if they made it or not. He was suspicious of all of them. With the amount of money that was on the line, he was sure that someone would break ranks.

On the other hand, he had already decided to break ranks. He would move his money in the next couple of days. After that there would be an assassination attempt. He would be out of the

Country recovering. With the money in hand he would never come back. He got the bulk of the money anyway.

Once gone in a country with no extradition treaty with Costa Rica, he would set the rest of his plan in motion. The documents had already been forged showing that the people behind the money had no involvement with the Colonel. He would not be left holding the bag. There was no trust in this game.

The Colonel was in it for himself. He would have each of them watched over the next couple of weeks to make sure no one was out of line. The Bank President had already been watched for the last couple of days. The Colonel knew that he was going to move money but did not know how fast. He had set it up so that if he left the island before the Colonel, he would not be tracked.

The meeting broke up without much fanfare. No one was watching so there was little interest in trying to sneak out. Most of the men just shuttled out the door and scattered. The Colonel lingered behind for one last word.

"It is over," he said to the Bank President. "But I will still be watching. This had better work. You have to know that if I go down, you will go down with me." He put his hat on and walked out the door. The Bank President stood in silence wondering if he would make it out with the money after all.

CHAPTER 24

The morning went by slowly. Final preparations were being made, and there were people darting back and forth. Regis, William, and Marcus had spoken before lunch to go over their part. William was the lead, but Regis, and Marcus, were to back him up. They could not come up with a specific distraction to go with, but they were told to just do anything that would last about ten minutes. That would be enough time for everyone to get in place. After that, they were to get the hell out any way that they could.

Regis spent the afternoon drinking to get ready for his part. Marcus ran around with The Pirate loading explosives for the trip. William was left with The Leopard who seemed to not be bothered by the circus around him. They sat watching the others gather up their things.

"Funny thing isn't it, Will?" The Leopard said while lighting up a cigarette. "Two weeks ago, you never knew I existed, and yet here we are." There was a pause, and a drag on the cigarette. "At first you don't come off as the type of person who takes chances. You show yourself as a cautious person who does not think he should get involved. But I know that is all bull shit." William turned his head to look at The Leopard a bit taken back by being called out by the old man.

"What is that supposed to mean?"

"Will, you're not as angry about all that is going on as you make out to be," he replied. "Sure, I bet you think about it a little longer than others, and that is not a bad thing. But you had the chance to get out of this long ago."

"I don't know how I would do that; I was already here," William said.

"No, I mean when the letter came," the Leopard replied. "You didn't have to come here yourself. You could have contacted a dozen different people including your friend's family, or the US government. They would have gotten involved, and no matter what your friend was up to, he would have been alright. No, you chose to travel halfway around the world, picking up another friend along the way, just to see if for yourself." The Leopard was hitting close to the mark, and William did not like it. He was grasping for some sort of retort but could not think of one.

"You see, this is what you wanted to happen. Maybe not exactly this, but you wanted something to happen." The cigarette was almost gone now, but it was sure to be replaced by another as William could tell the conversation was not over yet. "I talked to your friend Marcus, and he told me about you coming over to Italy. It is not a coincidence that you didn't become a lawyer and are now sitting on an island planning a jail break."

"You seem to have me all figured out," William said without anything in mind to contradict The Leopard.

"It's not very hard," he said. "So why don't you stop fighting it and just accept it." The Leopard stood up and walked away. William sat there thinking about what he had to say. The more he thought about it the more it seemed like a compliment.

The goal was to get everyone over there in three different groups. Marcus and The Pirate were in the first group with two others. They would take the explosives over to the island and get in position. The thinking was, if they did not make it into position, then it would be useless for the other to join the party. Regis would go with the second group, and William, the Leopard, and a driver were to go last.

William was the nicest dressed of them all. He and Regis were going to meet up after nightfall and go over there plan one more time. William hesitated to call it a plan at all. It only consisted of William going in the jail again and making a scene. He would demand to see Chris and go on and on about his status as an American something or other. Regis would translate but promised to act confused at points to make it last longer. Given his level of intoxication over the last few days, it would not take much to confuse him.

William stood on the dock as Marcus left on a boat. It was still mid-afternoon, but it would take hours to get everything in place. He thought that the best time to break them out was in the middle of the night. However, The Leopard told them that they needed a little help from the inside. Since that was the case things would have to go down a little before midnight. They had already coordinated it with those on the inside. William again would have to just go along.

The hours went by slowly as William sat outside The Leopards house. He said good-by to a nervous Regis and allowed himself to have a beer. Anything more he worried would compromise his ability to think on his feet. The Leopard came out with a drink of his own and sat down.

"You haven't told me what your part in all of this is," William said to him.

"I know," the Leopard replied.

"So maybe now would be a good time to do so."

"Does it really matter what I do?"

"It does to me," William said. "I want to know what is going on around me."

"That's the problem Will," the Leopard replied. "You think you always have to know everything. It is going to give you a heart attack one day. Relax, and let things happen." It was another non-answer from The Leopard. William took it yet again as a free life lesson.

"I don't really have anything to do," the Leopard said. "Pretty much I am just going along to see what happens." William looked surprised at the honesty. "Sometimes you don't have to have a specific job. You can just be there if someone needs you."

Relax was not something William would be doing for a while. It was almost time for them to leave, and his stomach was not doing too well. There was not much for them to take, other than themselves. William took a bag of clothes to dress up a bit when it was time for his part. It would be too hot to wear it all of the way there. He would end up a ball of sweat and dirt if he did. The Leopard carried nothing but a beer and most likely a couple of packs of cigarettes. When it was time to go the two made their way to the dock to find a boat waiting. It was only three of them in the boat as the sun slowly made its way over the water.

It was dusk when they made it to the island. Everyone else had started toward town, so it was just them. A car had been provided for their trip. William knew that there had to be more people involved because having someone's car waiting for them was not an easy matter. Somehow The Leopard had gotten three for this day alone. Without much fanfare they hopped in the car and started toward town. The road was bumpy, and slow, but they were in no hurry. It would take a little bit to get to town, so The Leopard leaned back to take a nap. William was wide awake thinking about what was going to happen next. The car ambled along the road, and William watched out his window hoping that he would not end up in the jail with Chris.

The driver had to turn the lights on as they entered the town. As usually there was not much going on. The car drove around the streets for almost twenty minutes before it stopped in front of a little bar in a part of town William had never seen. He did not know if the driving was to shake off anyone that might be watching, or if the driver did not know where he was going.

"This is our stop," said the Leopard refreshed by his nap. They got out of the car and headed inside. The bar was bigger than it looked on the outside. Since many of the buildings were connected it was hard to tell how much space each had.

They walked in with The Leopard in the lead. William did not see any of the other in the room. There were only two people sitting at the bar, and no one at the few tables scattered about the room. The Leopard went straight up to the bartender and started talking. The two seemed like long lost friends who were lost in a two-minute conversation.

"Everyone is fine," the Leopard said. "They are in the back." William walked to a small room in the back and found everyone seated around two tables. It was a ragged bunch taking down a few last shots of courage before heading out. Marcus was sitting with The Pirate speaking in hushed tones about what they were about to do. He had baled on going in with William and Regis and wanted to be where the action was. Regis was sitting at the other table looking like someone about to face the electric chair. William grabbed a beer and sat down. They had a little while to wait before each of the groups headed out. His would be the last.

Time went by slowly as they sat there waiting. Each group was to leave at a certain time. The first was to leave and take up a position outside one of the walls. The second was to do the same a little way away. William and Regis would leave last and make their way to the entrance of the building. At a pre-arraigned time, he would start to make a scene.

"Are you ready?" Marcus said as he came up beside William.

"Does it matter now?" William replied.

"I guess not," Marcus said. "I will see you later." Marcus shook William's hand and started out with The Pirate. They took with them bags of explosives to use against the walls. They carried canvas bags with straps and did not do a thing to disguise them. William knew that no one would stop them or ask questions in this town at this time of night.

About a half an hour later the second group got up to leave. William did not really know any of them, so he just gave a nod, and off they went. That left William, Regis, and The Leopard.

"So how do you think things are going now?" William asked The Leopard.

"Just as they should as best as I can tell," he replied.

"What do you think is going on inside the jail?"

"If we're lucky the guys on the inside have started to move into position and are doing what we told them to do."

"What was that?" William asked.

"They need to get the guards out of the two towers, and away from the blast side," he replied. "That way they can't see us setting up, and no one will get hurt in the blast."

"Nice thought to save life and limb," William said.

"No need to get anyone hurt," the Leopard replied. "We just want to get our guys out of there."

"I hope this works," William said to end the conversation. In a few minutes it would be his turn to get going. He went into the bathroom to change into the nicer clothes he brought. He worried about being a well- dressed American showing up around mid-night on a random day to demand the unauthorized release of a prisoner. He looked at himself in the broken mirror above the sink that he refused to touch. The young man looking back at him did not seem like someone that would participate in a jail break.

He walked out to find Regis sitting alone at a table. He looked like he wanted to throw up but would not let himself. William walked over and put his hand on his shoulder. It was time to go. They did not have to hurry. There was still a little time left before they would have to make their entrance. William wanted a little extra time in case anything went wrong.

They walked out into the night. There was not much of a wind, so the heat hung in the air. It did not help that William was dressed in long sleeves for the first time in weeks. He led the way toward the Detention Center. They were careful not to cross paths with anyone from the other groups. William walked along wondering what The Leopard was up to. It did not matter now. They were only minutes away from being inside. He could only hope that everyone else was ready. They turned the corner and could see the detention center ahead. No one was out on the streets. For some reason they seemed even quieter than usual.

CHAPTER 25

Chris had no idea what he was supposed to be doing. The slender man told him that at a certain time in the night he would come and get him. From there Chris was supposed to approach a guard tower and tell them they needed to leave so he could clean. The slender man assured him it would work even though it meant that Chris would have to get them to leave their post. There were never many guards on the night shift. It was hard to find people to sit around all night and babysit a bunch of guys asleep in cells. Therefore, the Detention Center was a skeleton crew late at night.

The time came and the slender man came to the cell. A guard was with him and opened the cell door.

"You will clean tonight," he said to Chris pointing to a brush and bucket. "Get out and follow him." Chris did what he was told and grabbed his stuff. He followed the slender man toward the stairs. The guard then left them to tend to the TV he had been watching. The two men climbed the stairs until they reached a door that lead them to the roof. The air was warm when Chris moved through the door. He had not been outside for a while, and for a moment just stood there taking in the openness of the space. He looked around and saw that the walls were covered in barbed wire, but other than that it was just the top of a building.

"You will go there," the slender man said as he pointed toward the far tower on the right. There were two towers on that side of the building. Each was manned by two guards.

"I will be in the other tower," he told Chris. "Just clean up a little bit until I come get you." Chris wondered how this was to lead to anything productive. "You must leave with me once I come get you. This is deadly serious. Do not question where we are going. Just follow me without delay."

Chris agreed to follow without question. He was too afraid to disagree. They parted ways and headed for their respective towers. Chris moved slowly so the slender man would reach his first. He wanted to see what happened when he got there. Chris walked slowly toward his tower watching his new friend enter the tower. Within seconds he saw the two guard leave the tower and start toward the stairs. He thought that was a good sign as he made his way into the tower.

"What are you doing here?" Asked one of the guards. He did not seem to care very much that an inmate just walked up without notice.

"I am here to clean," Chris said.

"Clean what?" The guard asked.

"I guess clean the tower." Chris hesitated a bit and told them. "I was told that guards no longer will have to keep up their workstations. The inmates have been put in charge of cleaning for them." The two guards looked at each other.

"Fine with me."

With that the two guards left without any more questions. Chris was left alone in the tower as the two guards made their way down the stairs. He did not know what to do at that point, so he started to clean. The slender man said he would come and get him when the time was right. Chris looked out of the window toward the other tower and saw that a red flag had been tied to the end of a mop and put out one of the windows. A few minutes later he saw the slender man come out of the tower, and hurry over to him.

"Come with me now!" It was a command that Chris knew he should follow.

William and Regis had made their way to the entrance of the Detention Center. William stopped for a moment at the doors and took a deep breath. He looked at Regis and pushed open the door. They walked into the waiting area and saw that there was no one in the room. No one was even manning the desk at the front. William walked up to the desk to see if he could get any-one's attention. He started to panic a little knowing that his only job was to draw as many guards to him as possible. There was not much time, and at the moment, he had drawn zero guards toward himself.

"What the hell to we do?" Regis asked.

"I guess we make some noise to get someone over here." William straightened his shirt and started to pound on the desk. At first, he did not pound loud enough, but soon he was hitting the desk with everything he had. His hand started to hurt from the repeated blows to the desk. Finally, a man walked out from the back eating a sandwich. William thought that he would be furious given the noise he was making. He walked up to the desk and looked at the two men standing there.

"What do you want?" He asked in Spanish. William looked at Regis, and Regis just looked back at him. William knew enough Spanish to know what he was asking.

"I am here because you are holding an American against his will," William started. "I demand to see him at this moment, and I will not leave until I do. This is the last time I will ask this."

He made a few wild hand gestures during the short speech for effect. The man just stood there looking at each of them. William looked at Regis, and he got the hint. Regis launched into the same speech, making the same hand gestures as William. The guard looked at him surprisingly still eating his sandwich.

"No, no visitors right now," the guard told them after Regis had finished.

"That is not acceptable! We will see him now!" William shouted this hoping to get some more attention. The guard still did not show much emotion and acted like he was just being misunderstood.

"It is too late, no visitors right now. Please come back in the morning," the Guard told him. William had yelled, demanded, and banged on the desk. Nothing seemed to be working. He decided it was time to go nuts. Since the guard did not understand English, he just started talking, and waiving his hands in the air. Regis started to tell the guard something in Spanish. William did not know what it was but hoped it would help.

Finally, the guard got up and went to the back. William hoped he would come out with more guards, and he did. At first, they just wanted to watch the show. William would jump around yelling in English at the top of his lungs. Regis would speak to them in Spanish warning them he was crazy, and something needed to be done. When William was up on a chair, he noticed a small glass incased control room behind the guard. It must have been some sort of control room.

More and more William yelled and jumped around. There were now about half a dozen guards in the room. William did not know how many he was supposed to get to come in, but he was almost out of time. A couple of the guards were getting tired of the noise and made their way into the waiting room. They told

Regis to tell William to stop, or he would be arrested. They just wanted them to go away. The guards approached William and said something to him in Spanish. He quieted down and looked at Regis.

"They said they just want you to go away," He told William. At that moment William saw that the guard in the control room had left his post and was standing by the desk watching. William jumped down and acted like he was heading toward the door.

Once he was at the desk, he made a quick jump over the it. The surprised guards did not know what to do. William raced toward the control room. He jumped inside and kicked the door closed. It was a bit of luck that the door locked automatically.

Regis stood in the waiting room stunned. That is when the guards lost it. They banged on the door shouting at William. Some of them were on their radios. Within seconds more guards surrounded the control room.

William looked around and saw that it was really only a small station that had a few video screens for cameras around the center. He did not know how long it would take them to get inside, but he knew it was not long. He looked down at the screen and saw two men run away from one of the outside walls of the Detention Center.

"Holy crap!" He said. He looked at Regis still standing out in the waiting room.

"Regis!" He said. "Down!" With that William hit the floor and covered his head. Within seconds there was a loud explosion. William wondered if the whole place would crash down on him. A few seconds later another loud explosion hit. Plaster fell from the ceiling. Everything that had been sitting on desks, or shelves, were knocked to the floor. William lay there covered in plaster and papers. The guards had been knocked off their feet. They were stunned and did not know what to do.

The first blast was set not far from where the main guard station was connected to the holding cells. William had done a masterful job. Almost all of the guards had headed up to the front to see what was going on. When the blast hit, it caved in the entrance to the holding area. The guards were trapped on the wrong side of the wall. The second blast had knocked a huge hole in the wall. Within moment inmates were being freed from their cells.

Smoke and dust filled the air when William opened the door. Most of the guards had either ran out the front door, as Regis did, or were trying to dig out the entrance to the holding area. No one thought to pay any attention to him as he staggered out the front door, and into the street. What he saw was chaos. People had come out of their homes, and police and guards were trying to make their way through the crowds to the detention center. William quickly mixed himself into the crowd and thought about what to do next.

Chris and the slender man had just made their way down to the holding area. They had looked around and found that all of the guards were making their way to the front. Chris had no idea why, but figured it was part of the plan. The slender man rushed Chris over to a corner right before the first blast hit.

Chris was thrown into the wall by the first blast. He tried to get up and move, but the slender man grabbed him. A second later a louder blast blew a hole in the opposite wall. Chris was flat on his face, and his ears were ringing. Dust had covered everything, and part of the wall and ceiling had collapsed against the main entrance.

He could see that there was a huge hole in the wall, and a couple of men were making their way through it. The slender man had run over the control panel and triggered the release of the cell doors. With a loud clang the doors of the cells started to open. The stunned prisoners did not know if they should stay or go. The slender man yelled out to them to get out while they could.

The inmates started to make their way over to the hole in the wall. In ones and twos they made their way outside. Within 90 seconds the whole place had been emptied. Chris did not know what awaited outside, but he knew that he could not stay. He followed the slender man out of the hole, and saw people scattered in all directions.

The streets were not well lit, and he had trouble finding his bearings. He did not have any idea of where to go. Just then the slender man grabbed him, and drug him into the forming crowd. People had come out of their homes to see what was going on. Chris could see that the police had arrived but were having trouble making it through the crowds.

"Where are we going?" Chris asked.

"You must follow me," the slender man replied. "There is more to do."

"What do you mean more to do?" Chris asked him. "We are out. The only thing we need to do is get out of here."

"No, there is more to do. It ends today. We are awfully close. You will see. It ends today." Chris could see the slender man smiling as he moved through the crowd. He had no idea what more there was to do, but decided his only option was to follow.

William had moved into the crowd, and slowly made his way from the detention center. More and more people were joining the crowd. He saw that some of them had bats, or clubs. Not knowing what these people were up to, he wanted to get as far away as possible. As William moved away from the center, more people were pushing him back toward it.

Every now and then, he saw a police officer in the crowd. Each time William saw a police officer it looked like he was being held by the crowd. Everywhere he looked he saw the crowd turning on the authorities. The Government was losing control. He pushed his way down the street and found a small opening on the corner. He leaned up against the wall to catch his breath and look back on what was going on. Fires had started around the detention center. At first William thought it must have been the blasts that started them, but then realized they might have been made by the crowd. He looked around and made out a face in the crowd. Pushing against the pulsating crowd, he saw Chris and another man making their way toward him.

"Chris!" He yelled waving his arms in the air. He probably could not have been heard for more than a few feet above the noise.

"Chris!" He yelled again as they got closer. There had been no reaction. They were only a few yards from him. He decided to get a hold of him. Pushing a few feet through the crowd he reached out and grabbed Chris's shirt, and pulled him down. Chris did not know what hit him. He was making his way through the crowd when someone pulled him down to the ground. He got up and saw that it was William.

"What in the hell is going on?" Chris asked William.

"No time to explain," William replied. "We need to get out of here."

"Follow us, he knows where to go."

CHAPTER 26

The blasts had awakened the Colonel from an early slumber. He quickly made it out to his balcony to see what was going on. Smoke rose from the detention center, and people were starting to come out in the streets. An attendant burst into the room and grabbed the nearest uniform for the Colonel. The Colonel turned to him grabbing the uniform. There were shouts coming from the street below. However, as typical of the Colonel, only the right uniform would do.

"This will not do," he said. "Go to the closet and get the one on the top shelf." Even in the midst of an event such as this, the Colonel was still preoccupied with which uniform he wanted to wear.

"Assemble the guards!" he yelled out the door. "I want to know what the hell is going on down there." He put on his uniform and made his way out of the bedroom.

Once downstairs the Captain of his guards stopped him at the door. He was out of breath and had a look of worry on his face.

"Sir, we can't go down there right now," he said.

"Why can't I?" The Colonel asked in an impatient voice.

"We think it could be dangerous," the Captain replied. "We don't know who is behind this, but there has been a bombing at the detention center.

"Assemble the combat team," the Colonel replied. "I will direct them myself."

"Sir, we are having trouble getting through to the detention center." The Caption told him. "The people of the town seem to be blocking the way." The Colonel knew what kind of trap that could turn into.

"I want the team assembled in five minutes, and we move out."

"Yes, sir."

The Colonel went back into his room and pulled a secret drawer out of the wall. In it stood several guns, and ammunition. The Colonel put on two holsters and loaded his guns. He took one last look out of the window and saw a growing crowd. He knew that if control was not established soon, it may never be established.

He made his way down the stairs, and out into a small court-yard. There he found assembled around 200 of the Colonel's own personal combat team. All of them were heavily armed with automatic rifles, and body armor. None of them seem very confident in what they were doing. Everyone could hear yelling coming from the streets just outside the compound.

"Now, men, we go to restore order in this city," he told them, wasting valuable time to give a speech none of them wished to hear. "You must now know that a fight has been brought to you. The glory of this island is now at stake. You are the last line of defense between mob rule, and democracy." With that he ordered the doors to the street opened. The Captain of the guards led them out. The Colonel hopped in an open car and moved to the middle of the formation. He wanted everyone to see who was in charge.

As they made their way down the streets the crowd started to part before them. Everyone stopped to look at the sight of hundreds of well-armed men marching down the street. It was only a couple of blocks to the detention center. Within moments the Captain of the guards made it to the entrance to the detention center. The crowd had quieted and moved to the side.

The Colonel pulled up in his open-air car to address the crowd. The crowd was growing by the minute. The people of the city came out with shovels and sticks and looked determined to stand their ground. The Colonel was unmoved. He knew that he only had to hold onto control for another day, and then could escape with enough money to last the rest of his life.

"This is an attack on our city!" He yelled to them. "I will not rest until those responsible for this are brought to justice. All of you must now choose. Those who are with us will live in peace. Those who are against us will be brought down with force." He looked around and found many scared faces in lines of troops he brought with him.

"Now go back to your homes, or this crowd will be dispersed by gun, and club." The combat team started to spread out up in front of the crowd. The crown moved back slowly but did not disperse. Only a few yards separated the end of the gun barrels, and the citizenry of the island. The crowd was calm, but at any moment seemed ready to explode. The combat team looked smaller and smaller as the crowd gathered around them.

"If they don't move, I want them fired upon," the Colonel said to the Captain. The Captain could not reply, and just gave a nod of his head. Sweat started to roll down his face as he looked out upon the crowd.

The Combat Team started to inch forward to move the crowds back from the street when a noise started to come from around the corner. It was a banging noise crossed with what they thought was singing. Everyone in the crowd stopped and turned to see what was going on. The combat team halted and looked around surprised. The Colonel was trying to see what was going on. When he looked up, he saw a massive crowd moving toward him. It was twice the size as the crown surrounding him now.

"They are coming this way!" A man in the crowd yelled, and the people went wild. The Colonel tried to yell commands at his troops but could barely be hear five feet away. The noise grew louder and louder. A mass of people came around the corner to join the crown already there. They were carrying clubs, and knives, and machetes. The crowd took up the whole street and was being cheered by the people they passed. This group was different. They were ready for a fight.

More noise came from behind the Colonel. He turned and saw a large group of people coming down the street behind them. This one was also massive and included homemade weapons of all sorts. The Colonel turned again, and to his horror the street in front of him filled with people. They had brought with them every weapon they could find. The combat team was trapped. The team moved slowly back toward The Colonel's car. The crowds were coming at them from three sides.

"Make a stand here!" Yelled the Colonel. The team just kept creeping back toward his car. Before long they were in a circle four deep around his car. Their guns were pointed towards the crowd. One wrong move by either side could end in disaster.

"Fire on them!" the Colonel yelled. Nothing happened as the crowd closed in on them. The team held their fire. The Colonel kept yelling fire, but no one would listen.

"Get me out of here!" he yelled at his driver as he grabbed the man by the back of his coat. "Drive through them if you have to but get me out of here."

The driver did nothing. They were surrounded by over two thousand people. Almost everyone in the town had to come, with even more coming in from the countryside. The Colonel could not believe it.

In the crowd stood William and Chris. The slender man had lead them to the crowd coming down the street. He knew it would be there. Once the crowd got to them the slender man took the lead and headed back toward The Colonel. All of the talk had turned to action. Now William and Chris stood in the middle of a sea of people. It was an expression of anger, frustration, and fear let out all at once. They wanted their island back, and they were going to take it by force if need be.

They moved to the side so they could get a better look at what was going on in front of them. They saw the crowd move toward the Combat team. The Combat team raised their guns. The Captain shouted something in Spanish. William did not know what it was, but all of the team dropped their guns to and moved away from the car. A great cheer went up from the crowd as the team members backed away and the crowd rushed forward. They swarmed the car before the Colonel had any chance to grab a gun. The last William saw of him, he was being taken away by the crowd, and his car used as a platform for the slender man. The Colonel was marched back to the ruble of the Detention Center he himself had created.

The slender man had managed to put it all together. The crowd was cheering their victory, as the members of the combat team were ushered to one side. The Colonel's car sat in the middle of the crowd abandoned. Soon the slender man jumped up on the car to another cheer from the crowd. He started talking, and the crowd silenced.

"Translate for me," William told Chris.

"Today we come together for the sake of our city, and island. For too long we have lived with fear, and tonight we say no more. From now on, the people of this island will be in control of their own destiny. Together, we form an unbreakable bond. One that will see us through the days ahead. Trust now one another and let us work together to make this island our own." He jumped down from the car and was surrounded by the crowd.

William and Chris made their way out of the crowd, which had now turned to a more celebratory mood. They wanted no part of it. This was not their island, and really not their celebration. William had been told a meeting point to go to after it was all over, but had a tough time remembering where it was. Since things had gone their way, it did not seem too important. Therefore, the two friends walked around the city meeting jubilant people celebrating their new freedom. The bars reopened and were full of happy patrons toasting the night's success. William and Chris could not resist stopping every now and then for a bottle or glass of whatever was being served. They had won and felt that a little bit of partying would not hurt.

Finally, they made it to the part of town William was told to go. There was a building that he was supposed to go to but could only remember that it was by a church. Everything else was fuzzy. They sat on the steps of the church to figure out what to do next when Marcus popped out of a door across the street.

"Are you guys looking for someone?" He said as he crossed the street. Chris and Marcus shook hands.

"I bet you weren't expecting me," Marcus said to him.

"How many of you are there?" Chris asked.

"Only a couple more. Come on in, the party started without you."

Marcus led them back inside the building. William found the guys standing around the room having a few beers. It was late, but everyone was still buzzed by the events of the night. Chris was overwhelmed by all the guys had done for him. He hugged a very drunk Regis and met all of the rest of the guys.

"Where is The Leopard?" William asked.

"He stepped out for a moment but will be back," Marcus said. William walked back outside to wait for The Leopard. Soon he saw a figure make his way toward the building. A lit cigarette hung from his mouth as he moved closed. The Leopard did not smile but looked at William as if to say we won. They stood on the sidewalk for a moment in silence.

"So, where were you?" William asked him.

"Do you have to know everything, Will?"

"No, but I thought it would be nice to know what your part was."

"Well, someone had to get this crowd together." William looked at him with admiration.

"So, you did this." The Leopard paused a moment and looked down at the ground.

"No, they did this," he said waving his hand vaguely in the air. "I just helped organize it." He went on to tell William how they had been planning something like this for a while. It just so happened that it came together when the guys had arrived. That is why he slipped out before William left. He was in charge of getting everyone ready to be out on the streets. They already had contact from someone inside. He had organized it before he went in. All the Leopard had to do was lite the fuse.

"I guess it worked out pretty well," the Leopard said to William.

"I guess it did."

CHAPTER 27

Almost a week had passed since the breakout, and the country was only starting to settle down. Around the world the little island made the news for several days. However, even the overthrow of a military dictatorship did not hold the attention of the worldwide public for long. After several days, with no mention of William and his friends, the news moved on to the ordinary cycle of Hollywood gossip and the new crime of the century. *So much for the informed public,* Marcus thought.

William and the guys were staying on at The Leopard's house for a few more days before heading out. They had watched the people of the island come together and try and take control of their own lives. However, it was time to get back to real life. Chris would head back to the States. He had talked to The Leopard about a job opportunity as a first-year professor at a college in Georgia. The Leopard knew someone there and would make contact. Regis would be heading back with him. He told William he'd had enough adventure for one lifetime and wanted to spend more time in the bars of the Crescent City.

All William could think about was getting back to Maria. Now that his friend was safe it was tough to think about anything but her. Before he left, they had thrown around the idea of getting married. William knew that he could not possibly find a better woman, than the brown-haired girl waiting for him on the other side of the pond. If she would take him, he knew that he could not let her go. After all he had been through a little domestic tranquility would not be so bad.

Marcus was torn between going back and staying on the island. He had spoken to a few people about hanging around to see what happens next. The Leopard told him that he could stay for a while and get the feel of the island. After that he might make a stop at home. He knew William would be there to take care of anything important.

The best part of the last week was hearing about what was happening on the island through the locals. News was slow that far out, but given its nature, this news traveled a bit faster than usual. Even though the public at large had moved on, the local population was just getting started. Jubilant men and women would pass by every so often with the latest news. The crowd had taken control of the city, and in effect the island. The police forces deserted The Colonel and joined the crowds. The mainland government was notified of what was going on, and immediately sent over police and administrators to restore order on the island. All government offices, and banks, were closed for two days.

A day later the news broke about the money in the bank. The bank president was caught at the San Jose International Airport trying to leave the country. On him they found over $500,000 in cash, and bank slips telling them where another couple of million had been stashed. He was led away, crying to everyone that it was The Colonel, and not him. Once they found the numbered accounts it did not take long for the police to gather up the group. They were all charged with money laundering, theft, and fraud. It did not seem like any of them would see the light of day for a very long time.

As for the Colonel. He had been taken by the crowd back to his detention center and tied to a chair. He firmly believed that they would kill him. The thought did cross the mind of a few, but the slender man found him, and made sure no harm came. They kept watch over him until the mainland authorities came to get him. He was led away in the last military uniform that he would wear in his life. His charges would be even more sever. In addition to the money laundering, fraud, and theft, they added conspiracy to commit murder, and attempted murder. There were more than enough combat team members willing to come forward and testify about The Colonel ordering them to fire on the crowd. The last William heard he had been taken to a maximum-security holding area in San Jose.

The guys had spent one more night at the split to celebrate everyone going their separate ways. Stories of that night were told over and over again. William knew they would be told many more times over the next few years. He had been assured that nothing would be done against those who participated in the prison break. The mainland government had issued blanket pardons for all involved. No questions were asked.

The people of the island reacted well and were ready to resume their normal lives. Things seemed to be in a good place. William was happy that he played a part. He had his fill of the middle latitudes and was ready to get back home. Now it was time to leave. As he stood in the darkness looking out over the water he wondered where life would take him next. All he knew was that he had a beautiful girl to live it with, and good friends to see him through.